TO
CLUTCH
A RAZOR

TO CLUTCH A RAZOR

VERONICA ROTH

TOR

TOR PUBLISHING GROUP

NEW YORK

TO CLUTCH A RAZOR

Copyright © 2025 by Veronica Roth

A Tor Book
Published by Tom Doherty Associates / Tor Publishing Group
120 Broadway
New York, NY 10271

www.torpublishinggroup.com

Tor® is a registered trademark of Macmillan Publishing Group, LLC.

EU Representative: Macmillan Publishers Ireland Ltd, 1st Floor, The Liffey Trust Centre, 117–126 Sheriff Street Upper, Dublin 1, DO1 YC43

The Library of Congress Cataloging-in-Publication Data is available upon request.

ISBN 978-1-250-85550-3 (hardcover)
ISBN 978-1-250-85551-0 (ebook)

Our books may be purchased in bulk for specialty retail/wholesale, literacy, corporate/premium, educational, and subscription box use. Please contact MacmillanSpecialMarkets@macmillan.com.

First Edition: 2025

Printed in the United States of America

10 9 8 7 6 5 4 3 2 1

For Alice,
who untangles the knots with me

Tonący brzytwy się chwyta.[1]

—a Polish saying

[1] A drowning man will clutch at a razor.

TO
CLUTCH
A RAZOR

A PRELUDE

Baba Jaga tugs the curtain back from the window with a gnarled hand. The reflection of the sun on the river is sharp as a knife. It cuts at her and she lets the curtain fall again.

Centuries of life have taught her there are certain patterns. Not just in other people's behavior, but in her own. She falls into them without meaning to, and her body knows before she does, remembering its old shapes. When she turns back to the Knight, she's young and sturdy, a warrior, with an as-yet-untested womb and a muscled arm.

If he's startled by the change in her, from old woman to young, he doesn't show it. But then, that's what she expects from this particular Knight. And though she reacts to him as if he was truly a Knight—a zealot with a holy mission to execute so-called monsters, such as herself— she knows that pattern doesn't actually apply to him. He chose a new path, one she's never seen walked before.

He asked her for destruction, and then, when that didn't suit . . . for transformation.

"And how are you settling into the new skin I gave you?" she says.

The last time she saw him, he had the look of someone who was creeping toward the edge of a cliff. Now he's unchanged in all the ways that would matter to a mortal—still tall, still strong, still with that dusty brown hair and eyes to match it—but in the ways that matter to an immortal, he's fundamentally altered. He looks shifty to her, like he might become something else entirely if she doesn't keep an eye on him.

"Ala is teaching me," he answers, and it's that accent, too, that carries her back to another time. He's fresh from the mother country, still on a guest visa, his consonants going still in his throat, his vowels too short.

"Ala," Baba Jaga repeats.

The experience of time is relative to age, with the minutes stretching long and lazy for a child and imperceptible for an adult, and so it might as well have been a second ago that she turned this Knight into a fear-eating nightmare creature. She amplified the few drops of zmora's blood that had crept into his veins until they drowned out the rest of him. That makes him a zmora, too, but perhaps . . . not all the way.

"Ah yes," Baba Jaga says, because it was only a second ago, after all, that Aleksja Dryja knelt on the rug not two feet from where the Knight currently stands. "Aleksja Dryja. A capable illusionist, I hear. But unimportant."

"Unimportant." He looks offended.

"A young Dryja who, up until you brought me the fern flower to cure her, was a ticking clock." Baba Jaga drums her fingers on her sternum, a habit she's passed along to some of her wraiths. The sound it makes is louder and higher than it should be, like her chest is hollow.

"The other Dryjas will not be so welcoming," she predicts.

"I don't expect to be welcomed."

"No, you don't, do you?" Baba Jaga laughs a little. "You expected death, and pain, and a life of suffering. You came to me for those things, thinking they would be your penance." She moves closer, her feet bare on the hardwood floor. As she walks toward him, the Knight's head bows further. "But soon you will get used to this new life, and you'll begin to want things you don't deserve. Acceptance, and trust, and yes—welcome."

She reaches out, and flicks beneath the Knight's chin to get him to raise it, to look at her.

"Already you want something you don't deserve: your sword. That's why you're here, isn't it? To inquire about your sword?"

In truth, she's the one who summoned him here. But not everyone comes when she calls—the wise know it's better to flee. Only the desperate turn up at her door, and she knows the source of this Knight's desperation.

It hums behind her, fixed to her wall. A longsword made of bone, bright white with a gilded hilt. It was made by magic, but not a magic Baba Jaga understands or respects—a magic that uses pain as currency, the magic of monster-hunting Knights of the Holy Order. She can feel the agony that brought it into being every time she walks past it, like a sour taste in her mouth, like an echo of a scream. It used to be buried in the Knight's back, formed by splitting his soul in half. And now it's hers—and by extension, *he* is hers, until he manages to earn it back.

He seems to know it, given how he stands before her like a soldier reporting to his commanding officer. Shoulders back, body still, eyes forward. She would enjoy it more if he didn't seem so damn *sad* about it. She can't tease someone who's yielded so completely.

"Yes, I . . ." The Knight looks down again. "You said I could get it back, for the right price. So I am here to ask what that price is."

"And what is the cost to you, exactly, if I keep it in my possession? Do you even know?"

He hesitates. She isn't sure how a Knight reacts when parted from their soul sword. She knows they can feel where it is, and they can use that feeling to track it. She knows it's not pleasant. But that's the extent of her knowledge.

"So far, the cost is . . . pain," he admits, after a moment.

"But you don't really care about pain, do you?" She tilts her head. "You believe it's no more than you deserve. Perhaps you even crave the punishment. So what do you care if the sword lives in my apartment?"

"I . . ." He frowns. Looks away. "It's more than that.

The Holy Order believes that if your sword can't be integrated with your body after you die, you will . . . wander the earth forever, neither alive nor dead."

"The *Holy Order* believes," she repeats. "And what do you believe?"

The Knight hesitates again. "I don't know."

"You should maybe find someone who does," Baba Jaga says. "It may give you some urgency that you currently lack."

"Do *you* know what will happen to me if I don't get it back?"

He should have asked from the start. Foolish boy.

"I have suspicions," she replies. "But whatever the truth is, I know it's not good to walk around with only half a soul."

The Knight swallows hard. He nods.

"You're in a terrible bargaining position," she says. "You come here with nothing but that tragic face, appealing to my merciful nature—*Oh, this Knight who would rather suffer and die than kill another monster, take pity on him, Babcia*—well, let me see how deep my well of mercy is today, shall I?"

She closes her eyes, and she feels herself shifting, hunching beneath the weight of time, her hair shivering as it turns dry as a corn husk and her skin softening over her bones. She has seen so many things, and death is one of them. And where there has been death, there have also been *Knights*.

Knights, their palms stained red, their eyes glinting red, their swords dripping red blood onto the hard ground.

Knights, chasing her brothers and sisters, daughters and sons, into the ancient woods of her old home.

Knights carving wounds into their own flesh to curse her kind with bloodthirsty crows or flesh-hungry wolves.

Knights who take every powerful symbol they find to twist it and warp it into their own.

Knights who crave death, and seek it, and cling to it like an oath.

"You were named for the harvest," she says to him, and she hears it, the way her voice deepens as she allows time to rush into her body again. It's so heavy, time. Easier, really, to keep it at bay, like a dog she has to keep nudging away from the front door with her foot every time she opens it.

"You were named for the harvest, and harvest you will." She looks at him. He doesn't look well. The skin under his eyes is almost purple. "Thirty-three bones made the sword that you used to slay the innocent, and to earn them back, you will bring me thirty-three swords drawn from the spines of the dead."

"You . . ." He almost whispers it. "You want me to kill thirty-three Knights?"

"Not just thirty-three Knights. You will begin with the one you call Babcia."

He stares at her, his eyes wide.

"Whatever one sows, that he will also reap," Baba Jaga

says. "Your grandmother sowed you. And you, my Knight, have sowed nothing but death."

She almost expects it, the way he goes to his knees. The posture of a supplicant comes to him too easily; he knows, too well, that he has nothing to offer but himself. A meager thing indeed.

He bows his head, and says, "Please."

Baba Jaga's bones ache. The light of the setting sun is orange, and acrid as the fruit that shares its color. She prefers night.

"I know . . ." His voice cracks. "I know they're . . ."

"You know they're what? Murderous? Violent?"

"Monsters," he supplies. "I know they're monsters. But a man can love a monster."

Kościej, something inside her whispers.

She remembers. She has loved a great many monsters, and Kościej was the greatest of them. In some ways he reminds her of the man kneeling in front of her. His soul displaced. His nature still undecided. Crooked and shrouded in darkness. But unlike this creature who begs her for mercy, Kościej knelt for no one.

"A man can love a monster, yes," she says. "And a man can also kill the things he loves."

"It would destroy me, to do what you ask."

"And you think I should care?" Something fierce rises up inside her, a memory self she hasn't encountered in some time. She grits her teeth so hard her jaw aches, and says, "Destruction is what you came to me for, Knight!"

A strong wind blows through the herbs that hang in dried bundles from her ceiling, blows through the pages of the books she's left open on tables and desks, here and there and everywhere, and it whips through the Knight's hair and clothes like it's fighting to tear him apart.

"Killing is all you're good for!" she shouts over the tumult.

The wind blows the Knight back, so he's cowering on the floor at her feet, an arm curled over his head. Bones sail through the air and tapestries flap against the walls and jars tumble from their shelves and crash, spilling eyeballs and dried tongues and rare powders across the hardwood.

"So kill the guilty instead of the innocent, for once," she says. "Or suffer the consequences of missing half your soul, whatever they are. Those are your choices, and don't you dare think them unfair."

She nudges time back with the toe of her shoe. The weight disappears from her shoulders, from her bones. Her skin tightens over muscle. She's young again, and a warrior again, and the air is calm.

The Knight is still cowering on the floor, windblown and terrified.

"Get out of my sight," she says.

She turns away from him, and tugs the curtain back to look at the river. The sun is still too bright on the water, but she lets it burn dark spots into her vision for a few seconds.

When she turns again, the Knight is gone.

A FAMILY MEAL

When Dymitr was a child, he often waited in the weapons room for his uncle to come back from a hunt.

Always his uncle, not his parents—because his mother, Marzena, liked to greet with admonishments, and his father, Łukasz, was unpredictable, at turns either kind or vicious. Uncle Filip, though, was ruddy-cheeked and sly; he took coins out of Elza's ears and taught Dymitr how to whistle with a piece of grass between his thumbs, and when Dymitr's older brother teased him for being too sensitive, too *soft*, Filip called him off.

So Dymitr would sit on the stone bench at the edge of the weapons room, his legs swinging, and wait for Filip to return. When he did, Filip's hands were always bloody, and his face was always smeared with dirt. He would offer Dymitr things piece by piece to be returned to their places: spare knives that hadn't been used in the hunt, and the armored vest, and his heavy boots, which always needed to be cleaned. He didn't talk much, after, but Dymitr didn't mind the quiet. And he didn't mind scrubbing Filip's boots, either.

Most of the time, the bone sword was sheathed by the time a Knight came home, so Dymitr's first glimpse of one came when he was ten years old, and Filip turned away from him to change his shirt. Filip went out on missions often, which meant he drew his sword often, so it was close to the surface of his skin. So close that Dymitr could see every ridge of the golden hilt, and every centimeter of the bone blade, standing out from Filip's back.

It was an honor to become a Knight. Not everyone in the family did. Not everyone had the constitution for it, as his grandmother liked to say. And the people of the village—the ones who were in the know—treated Knights like royalty. Knights always got to go to the front of the line at the butcher shop, always got extra cakes at the bakery. Even the unruly teenagers who played soccer in the field behind the old factory went silent and still at the sight of them. Knights were like old heroes of legend come to life.

So the sword, such an integral part of becoming a Knight, should have left Dymitr awestruck. Instead, he shuddered at the sight of it bulging from Filip's shoulders like a tumor. He wanted to look away from it, but he couldn't stop staring until Filip put a clean shirt on to cover it. Then Filip turned around and looked at Dymitr standing there with bloody boots in hand.

"You haven't seen one before?" he asked.

Dymitr swallowed. He felt nauseated. "Not up close."

Filip clicked his tongue, disapproving. "Your parents

have been neglecting your education." He sat on the stone bench next to the door. "Come. Ask your questions."

Curiosity wasn't always rewarded in Dymitr's family, so the invitation to ask whatever questions he liked was a rare one. He stood in front of his uncle, his fingers twisted together in front of him.

"Does it hurt to draw it?"

"Yes," Filip said steadily.

He had a thick beard, gray in places, and neatly trimmed. There was a scar through his left eyebrow—a big, crooked one that made his skin pucker and ripple.

"Does it hurt to sheathe it?"

"Yes."

"Then why . . ." Dymitr furrowed his brow. "Why not just leave it here in the weapons room, then collect it next time you go out on a mission?"

"Well, for one thing, it tugs at you when you're separated from it, so you can always find it. Annoying. And for another . . ." He shrugs. "It's good to always have a weapon with you. Monsters don't only attack when we hunt them. They can creep into our houses, slip into our bedrooms while we sleep. Infest our bodies and minds, feed on our blood. The sword is with me always, so I'm never defenseless against them."

No one ever softened things for Dymitr, or any of the children in the family. Monsters were everywhere, pain was inevitable, and only the strong could survive both.

"The sword is a tool," Filip said. "But it's also a treasure—because it's hard won, understand?"

Dymitr never had much. Not because his family couldn't afford it, but because they didn't believe in certain indulgences. Nothing without purpose: a child's bow-and-arrow set, for learning archery; a chessboard, for learning strategy; a survival kit, for learning to be resourceful. He and his brother and Elza had a fort in the woods, built from fallen logs, where they went to start small fires and set traps and identify mushrooms. They had tournaments with the rest of the cousins that were half playful, half serious. They quizzed each other with questions that sounded like the first parts of jokes, but weren't. *What is most commonly misidentified as a strzyga? What do you call a banshee in Germany? In what country can you find an oni?*

He was used to his most valuable possessions having purpose. And that purpose was always related to monsters.

"How . . ." Dymitr was almost afraid of the question, but he asked it anyway. "How are they made?"

"We do it in here," Filip said, gesturing to the weapons room before them. "You'll lie on a table, face down. There will be four Knights with you. One will be your mentor, when you get one. One will speak the words of the ritual. And the other two . . ." He looked at Dymitr, assessing. "The other two will hold you down."

Dymitr's mouth went dry.

"Your mentor will take their own blade and cut into your back. Right down the center."

Dymitr imagined it like carving a chicken: his skin crispy beneath the blade, clear juices bubbling up from that first cut. He shuddered.

Filip continued, "Then they'll cut into themselves, and let their blood spill into the wound. The words of the ritual are spoken, and then . . ." He swallowed hard. "It will hurt. It will feel like every bone in your body is breaking. It will feel like a thousand deaths. You'll pass out. But then, when you wake . . . you'll be twice as powerful as before."

Filip reached out and put his hand on Dymitr's head. He gave him a serious look.

"Don't fear pain, Dymek," he said. "Fear . . . losing your purpose, losing your family, losing yourself. Those things are worse than pain."

Dymitr chose this coffee shop because it has two exits.

Well, and because the baristas are good at latte art. There's one, Zuri, who always draws something special for him. Most of the time, she just makes beautiful patterns, but once it was a swan, once it was a seahorse, once a four-leaf clover. Her cheek dimples when she smiles. And she's always stressed, which he's now realizing is a source of appeal . . . given that he now eats fear.

He sits by the window, equidistant from each exit, and waits for John to arrive.

There are American families of Knights, of course. One

for each region. Like the country itself, their traditions are cobbled together from other places, a patchwork-quilt version of Knighthood that Dymitr's family always liked to sneer at . . . despite the fact that they themselves had pieced their practices together from Polish tradition and Kashubian and Jewish, from Orthodoxy and Catholicism and paganism. The hypocrisy stands out to Dymitr now, though it never did before.

John is slim and blond and walks with forearm crutches. His skin is a few shades darker than Dymitr's, like he recently spent some time in the sun. When he spots Dymitr sitting by the window, he grins, and Dymitr has to wonder how John identified him so quickly. The coffee shop is crowded with stressed-out students hunched over their laptops, spandex-clad yoga students with mats tucked under their table, and two older men playing cards.

"Process of elimination," John says, like he heard Dymitr's thoughts. Once he's seated, he leans the crutches up against the window. "You must be Dymitr."

He makes the name sound clumsy. He offers Dymitr his hand, and Dymitr shakes it. He's tense, even though John never became a Knight, so he can't use magic to see what Dymitr really is. From what he's heard, John makes up for his lack of magic in other ways. He's adept at following digital footprints—increasingly important these days—and has a knack for spotting things others don't.

"A pleasure to meet you," Dymitr says.

"I'm glad our schedules overlapped. I'm only here for a

couple days. Have you tried a hot dog yet? I'm told I need to surrender to the full cadre of toppings, but I'm suspicious of the neon-green relish."

Dymitr was already aware that John talked a lot, but hearing it in person is another thing entirely.

"I haven't, no," Dymitr says.

"You Eastern Europeans always have this aura of profound gloom, you know that?" John waves at Dymitr's face. "Or maybe Americans are just obnoxiously chipper. That world-famous optimism, right? Not so much to be optimistic about these days, of course—"

Though Dymitr didn't ask, John launches into a summary of the situation across the Midwest. The region is spotted with so-called monstervilles—small towns full of creatures of all varieties who realized they could band together to keep themselves safe. And that's not even accounting for the new influx of *things* from all around the world.

"Not just your old-world standards anymore," John says, with an exaggerated wince.

"The world is the same age no matter where you go," Dymitr replies. "Just because it's new to you doesn't mean it's new."

John blinks at him, like Dymitr was just spouting philosophy instead of a simple fact.

"Suppose you're right about that," he says with a shrug. "Now what was it you wanted to meet about? Something about . . . *swords*?"

"I heard you're the Moore family historian," Dymitr says. "I wondered if you'd ever come across information about what happens when a Knight is parted from their sword."

Zuri, of course, chooses that moment to carry John's latte over to their table. The face of an owl stares up at Dymitr from the mug, and he feels a bubble of hysterical laughter in his chest as he thinks of Niko, his strzygoń . . . not-quite-boyfriend, and the second form he can shrug on and off like a jacket.

Zuri winks at Dymitr, who manages a weak smile, and tells them to holler if they need anything else, one of those folksy phrases that sounds wrong if Dymitr tries to say it in his accent.

Once Zuri is gone, John leans over the table, conspiratorially.

"As a matter of fact, I have," John says. "And a more recent account than you'd think. My great-grandfather's death was a bit of a family mystery for most of my life, right? In our family records he was a beast of a man, big and strapping, killed a whole bunch of game"—*game* is what they call their work in public, in case anyone is listening to their conversation—"and then one day, poof. Gone. No account of what got him, if anything. Weird stuff. But my grandfather, he left behind a lot of old journals when he passed, and guess who has two thumbs and got tasked with reading through all of them?"

He gives Dymitr a double thumbs-up, and then points back at himself.

"*This* guy," John says. "Anyway there was a record of him losing his sword in a fight against one of our fearsomest feathery friends—" Dymitr thinks that means strzygas. "But the owl flew the coop instead of sticking around to kill him, with his sword in hand. He tried like hell to find her, and so did a few of the others, by all accounts— but no dice. And then things took a turn."

"A turn?"

"Well, for the first few weeks, he was in pain—body aches, and constant thirst and hunger that never seemed to be sated. No big deal for a man of his constitution, right?" John shakes his head. "Well, then he started seeing a different owl, one he'd brought down a few years before. The family thought, you know—a curse. A haunting. A hallucinogenic poison. Whatever. And then he saw other things. Old game. Crows—" Those were zmoras. "And wolves—" Werewolves. "All kinds of things. An entire menagerie. They didn't replay old memories, or anything, they just talked to him nonstop. Taunted him, refused to leave him alone. Eventually there were so many of them he couldn't hear anyone over the noise. He just stayed in his room with his fingers in his ears."

"And he died from it?"

John shakes his head. "No, it didn't kill him. Not directly, anyway. He did that himself. Couldn't take it anymore, left a note and everything. That's why there was no official record of it—a Knight's not supposed to destroy himself, right? He's supposed to take something else down with him."

As a child, one of the first things Dymitr understood about Knights was that there were good ways for a Knight to die and bad ways. Dying because you were stupid or scared or didn't prepare for the work at hand adequately or lost your nerve in the middle of a fight, those were shameful ways to die. But dying because you were saving someone else, or because you were fighting something especially fierce or deadly—those were good deaths.

No Knight hoped to live a long life; they hoped for a good death.

"I guess it makes sense, you know? You can't just walk around without half your soul without suffering some consequences," John says. "So why the sudden interest? Someone you know misplace theirs?"

"I know someone whose sword is in the wrong hands," Dymitr says quietly. "Though he knows exactly where it is, it will be difficult to get back. He wanted to know how urgent it was that he do so."

John's smile fades.

"Tell your friend that it's urgent. From beginning to end, it was only a few months for my great-grandfather. And it got bad much sooner than that."

Dymitr looks out the window at the cars driving past. At the construction workers setting up orange traffic cones on Irving Park. At the woman walking her corgi past a hair salon and stopping by the door for the stylist to toss a treat.

"Thank you for your help," he says to John distantly. "I have to go."

John's hand brushes his as he stands, an attempt at comfort that Dymitr doesn't acknowledge.

※

Dymitr stops at the top of the stairs and leans against the wall. The scents of the stairwell are overwhelming. Rubber boots. Sweaty feet. Petrichor. Wet carpet. Soggy paper from the mail Ala must have brought in earlier—the mailbox has a leak in it. Whatever food the neighbors had delivered. He closes his eyes and takes a deep breath through his nose. Basil and peanuts—Thai food from the place down the street, if he had to guess.

The smells distract him from the ache in his chest. He rubs his sternum absently, and unlocks the door with the spare key. He's been staying at Ala's place since his transformation. *Just until I get my bearings,* he promised her. She just rolled her eyes, like he was being ridiculous.

The apartment is too small for both of them. He sleeps on the couch, and his feet hang off the end of it. There's no room in the refrigerator for both his milk—whole—and her milk—1 percent—so they compromise by buying 2 percent. Just this morning she made him get out of the shower early so she could use the toilet. They don't know each other, not really, but the cramped space has forced an intimacy neither of them is quite comfortable with yet. He can tell it would be better if he was gone, and also that Ala is too stubborn to tell him so.

She's in the kitchen when he arrives. She hasn't gotten her hair cut in a while, so it's starting to curl behind her ears. She's wearing an old gray T-shirt with holes at the collar seams. When he tries to peek at what's on the stove, she blocks it with her body and grins at him. "Tell me what it is."

She seems to love this game.

"It's ramen," he says.

"Not specific enough."

"It's the Sapporo brand," he says. "You put carrots and broccoli in it. And an egg."

She grins and steps aside, revealing an old pot—red, with white flowers painted on it—full of noodles. "Want some?"

"Do you even need to ask?"

She takes another bowl out of the cupboard, and starts ladling soup into it. Zmoras don't need to eat much regular food, since fear makes up the bulk of their diet. A meal every few days, maybe. But he still appreciates how generous she's been with food and money while he looks for work.

As she hands him the bowl, she says, "I'll never get tired of that, I swear. Your nose is so much better than mine."

"A pity my illusions are so much worse." Ala has been

trying to teach him the art of it, but his illusions, when he even manages to conjure them, have no strength. They flicker in and out, they go hazy at the edges. Sometimes they don't even look like what he's picturing.

They sit at the rickety yellow table in the corner. It's only big enough for two people, and even then, his knees knock against hers when he sits down, so he turns sideways in his chair. He lets the steam from the soup envelop his nose, and closes his eyes. Salt. Carrot. Chicken bouillon. Metal, from the pot. Wood, from the spoon. His chest aches.

"I saw there's a showing of *I Know What You Did Last Summer* tomorrow night at the Crow," he says casually.

Ala hesitates. The Crow Theater is a zmora operation, run by Ala's family, the Dryjas. They play scary movies as a kind of fear buffet in disguise. He hasn't been there since his transformation—hasn't actually met *any* of the other zmoras in Ala's life. It's as if she doesn't want them to know he exists.

Or maybe as if she doesn't trust him around them. And really, can he blame her, after all the things he's done—not just to her people, but to *her family,* specifically?

"I didn't mean you should take me," he clarifies. "I meant you should go alone. Get some . . . junk food."

It's hard for him to get used to, thinking of other people's fear as a meal. But he can tell when he gets a good one. He feels sated, almost giddy. The more fear he eats, the more fearless he becomes. Reckless, like he could climb a tall building or leap off a bridge. He was alarmed by this at first, but it's gotten easier to control.

The first few days, he went searching for it. There are some places where people are always afraid. The first place he went was the hospital waiting room, where he sat steeped in anxiety for hours. The next day, he went to a sports bar, where some kind of important fight was on every television set. There, he found a blend of anxiety, apprehension, eagerness. All shades of fear.

So there's been no shortage of food, even though he hasn't been to the Crow.

"I'm being silly," Ala says.

"You're not being silly," Dymitr says. "You don't want to tell a family of zmoras that you're harboring a Knight. There's nothing silly about that."

Ala stabs at her soup with her spoon, even though it's an ineffectual tool for stabbing. She scowls at him. "You're not a Knight. And you saved my life. I just need some time to—"

Some time to believe I've really changed, he supplies, and the thought twists his insides. And really, should she believe it? He's done very little to earn her trust, and a great deal to break it.

Dymitr touches her wrist, lightly. She tenses at the contact, and he can't tell if it's because a part of her is still afraid of him, or if she just doesn't like to be touched. Either way, he withdraws his hand.

"Just because I helped you with that curse doesn't mean

you owe me something," he says. "And it doesn't mean everything's all better now."

He says it too darkly, thinking about his sword, fixed to Baba Jaga's wall.

Ala stares down at her soup. She brings a spoonful of the broth up to her mouth, and blows on it. Then she asks, without looking at him: "What did she say?"

She doesn't need to specify who *she* is. There's only one *she* that Ala would be reluctant to name: Baba Jaga.

"The price of my sword is thirty-three deaths. One for each vertebra." And he chokes a little as he adds: "Beginning with my grandmother."

Ala lets the soup drip back into the bowl. She doesn't look surprised. The look in her eyes is unreadable. "I thought it might be something like that."

"And I spoke to an old contact about what will happen to me if I don't pay that price," he says. "It's . . . bad."

"Death?"

"Madness."

They're both quiet for a while. She knows better than anyone what it is to inch closer and closer to losing yourself, but he doesn't want to bring it up—doesn't want to suggest that it's the same thing.

They start eating in silence. Ala has the furrowed brow she gets when she's thinking something through. And Dymitr, well. He's used to eating when he feels terrible. After every mission. Before every mission. And eventually . . . between every mission, too. He hasn't felt ease at the dinner table since he was a child. Since before he split his soul.

"My parents didn't act like parents," he says, when the silence has gone on too long for him to bear. "They preferred to be . . . working. Away from each other, and away from us. So my grandmother raised me instead." He can't bring himself to look at Ala. "She was the first person to tell me she loved me."

Ala reaches out and puts her hands on top of his. He only realizes then that he's been clenching his hands together so hard he's lost the feeling in his fingers.

"I know she deserves to die," he says. "But I would rather give my own life than be the one to do it. I would rather lose my mind."

"Okay," she says. "Okay."

She coaxes his hands away from each other, and presses them flat to the table. Then she picks up their bowls and carries them to the sink.

"We'll think of something," she says. "We're not giving up yet. Not even close."

He doesn't reply.

A NEW HUNT

Lidia Kostka, matriarch of the Kostka strzygas, traces the edge of her glass of whiskey with her fingertip. Assembled around her are her favorites of the Kostka cousins—which is to say, the ones Nikodem Kostka is most wary of. Their owl eyes shine at him from every direction, some yellow, some black, and some, like his own, burnt orange, like the edge of a flame. At the slightest hint of a threat from him, they could all change into their hidden forms, taking on beaks and talons and feathery wings.

But Niko isn't here to threaten anyone. He was summoned, so he came, even knowing how . . . *displeased* Lidia and the others must be. Just a few weeks ago, he foiled their attempts to steal the mythical fern flower from Dymitr and Ala, and Lidia hates when people interfere with her plans.

They're beneath the boxing arena, in the building that's a factory by day, its supranormal elements cloaked by magic. Specifically, they're in the bar where Niko pulled off Dymitr's fingernail to use it to aid their escape. The low red lamps are dim enough that he can't quite see his cousins' expressions, but he can guess they're full of malice.

"I want to apologize," he says to Lidia, even though he doesn't.

"Whatever for?" she says.

She's small and waiflike, Lidia Kostka, with that kind of pale skin that's borderline translucent. Like a woman—no, a *girl,* really—from an impressionist painting. Her dress is from another time, a white, fringed shift that makes her almost glow in the dark. She's far older than she looks, and far older than he is. He needs to be careful of her.

But he's not defenseless. The zemsta oath—the oath he took to seek vengeance against the Knights of the Holy Order—has its advantages. Chief among them: he's always capable of substantial magic, thanks to the sacrifices he's made for his people. He won't be quick to provoke the Kostkas again, but Lidia won't be quick to provoke *him,* either.

"I owed Aleksja Dryja a debt. She helped a friend of mine," Niko says. "That's why I prevented you from taking the fern flower. I didn't enjoy it, but it had to be done."

"That didn't sound like an apology to me," Lidia says. She looks over her shoulder at the Kostka cousin closest to her, a tall woman with a perpetual grin who's perched on the edge of the sofa, her arm draped over the back. "Did it sound like an apology to you, Iga?"

"More like an excuse," Iga replies. "Spoken in an unrepentant tone, no less."

"It was an *explanation,*" Niko says. "I haven't gotten to the apology yet."

"An explanation for why you chose a zmora and a mortal over your own family?" Lidia's voice is smooth and pleasant. "I'm afraid that if a simple debt is your explanation, your apology is bound to be insufficient."

"Then maybe you can just tell me how I can make amends. I'm eager to make it up to you."

"As it happens, that's why I've summoned you here, my dear boy," she says. "I have a special target in mind for you."

His job, as zemsta, is to hunt down members of the Holy Order on behalf of his people—and on behalf of all not-so-human people, really, since they've all been wronged by Knights at one point or another. He takes specific requests from anyone with a sincere desire for vengeance. They tell him who they lost and how, and they give him all the details they have about the Knight who took their loved one from them. Then he finds them and eliminates them.

This is not a request. This is a demand.

"Oh?" he says. "Which Knight has particularly offended you?"

Lidia smiles, enough to show off yellowing teeth. Though Niko's own smile stays plastered on his face, fear spikes in his chest. If Lidia is smiling, this is going to be bad.

"I think it's time someone does something about Brzytwa," she says.

Very bad.

"You want me to hunt the Razor," he says.

Not all Knights get a nickname. Only if they're particularly prolific, cruel, or long-lived. The Razor is all three, a monster among monsters, one of the most ferocious Knights alive. At the mention of the name, the entire room goes still, like they've spotted a predator and are contemplating taking flight.

"Yes," Lidia says. "Does that trouble you? I have the utmost confidence in your abilities, Niko. You haven't failed us yet."

If I had, I'd be dead, he thinks. You don't just *fail* to kill a Knight—you die trying. That's the way every zemsta before him has gone: bloody and sudden.

If Lidia has decided his next target is the Razor, it's because she wants him dead.

"Trouble me?" he says, and he forces an even broader smile. "Of course not."

The gangway between Ala's apartment building and its neighbor is so narrow the brick walls scrape Niko's shoulders as he walks. Dymitr's guitar case bumps against his back. He nudges the gate open and steps around the herb garden to the back stairs.

As he climbs, he sends Dymitr a text message. *Out back. Come get your bow.*

At first, after Dymitr's transformation, Niko came by every day. Though they were little better than strangers, they'd all gone through something intense together, told each other things they hadn't told anyone, and it didn't feel right to just return to his normal life after that. But eventually, once Dymitr was set up with a burner phone and a little stack of clothes fresh from the nearest resale shop—the T-shirt with three wolves and a moon on it was Niko's favorite, though it smelled musty even to his average strzygoń nose—Niko had to admit there was no reason for him to hang around quite so much anymore. He lives across the city, after all.

But he's leaving tomorrow, so he wants to see Dymitr before he goes. Just in case. Danger is an inevitability for a zemsta, oath-bound to hunt the Holy Order in pursuit of vengeance. And this mission in particular . . .

Well.

He shrugs off the guitar case and leans it up against the half-rotten table Ala keeps on her back porch, then perches on the edge of it, next to the pot of petunias. They're the pink-and-white-striped kind. Hideous.

The back door opens, and Dymitr steps out of the apartment, his feet bare, wearing gray sweatpants and a white T-shirt that's too big for him. His hair is mussed. Niko wants to run his hand through it, but instead he just crosses his arms and says, "Dobry wieczór."

It's intentionally formal. *Good evening*, like they're from another time.

As if he can't quite stop himself, Dymitr steps closer—too close. He touches the side of his nose to Niko's jaw and breathes in. The first time he did this was in Ala's kitchen, right after he woke as a zmora, and Niko assumed the fascination with his new nose would fade, in time. So far, it hasn't—not where Niko is concerned, anyway. And he's not complaining. There's something . . . appealing about the way Dymitr takes those deep breaths of his skin. About how attentive he is.

Niko is counting on it today. Anna O'Connor ran a perfumed finger across Niko's shoulder at the boxing ring earlier, and he wants to see if Dymitr can smell it—and if he can, Niko wants to feel Dymitr's jealousy. He's a strzygoń, after all, and anger—and all its many shades—is his sustenance.

He can tell when Dymitr notices it, his head dropping to Niko's shoulder as he breathes in again, only . . . there's no cold spill of jealousy. No anger at all, in fact.

"Well, that's disappointing," Niko says, though he runs a hand through Dymitr's hair anyway, scratching at his scalp with the blunted-talon fingernails of a strzygoń in human form.

"What is?" Dymitr says, his head heavy against Niko's shoulder.

Niko was the one to point out to Ala that Dymitr was in pain. He's good at bearing it, so the signs were subtle, but the way even the briefest comfort—Niko's fingers in his hair, for example—makes him sag with relief, the way he rubs at his chest when he thinks no one's paying attention . . .

"I have someone else's perfume all over me, and you don't feel even a little bit jealous."

Dymitr looks up at him, an eyebrow raised. "You *want* me to be jealous?"

"Can you blame me for being curious what it feels like?" Niko smiles a little. "I am what I am, after all."

"Some people would call that a red flag."

"The fact that I can turn into a deadly monster in an instant should be a much bigger, redder flag."

Dymitr gives him a small smile in return. There's a crease between his eyebrows that Niko wants to smooth away. So he does, pressing his thumb right between Dymitr's eyes, then brushing the tension away with a sweep of his hand.

"I'm not jealous because I'm not entitled to you," Dymitr says.

It should be reassuring, maybe, or noble, but to Niko it only seems sad. Sometimes anger is entitled and jealous, but sometimes it rises up to demand what you feel you deserve. And Dymitr feels he deserves nothing and no one.

Niko doesn't know what to say, so he kisses Dymitr instead. Lightly, at first, but soon Dymitr's hands are clutching at the lapels of Niko's jacket, and Niko is pressing Dymitr back into the brick wall. He tastes something familiar—the old, dusty mints that his grandmother keeps in a dish outside of her apartment—but he brushes that recognition aside in favor of . . . *this,* this frantic need to burrow under Dymitr's skin and stay there forever. He leans closer, pinning Dymitr against the wall with his own body, to feel the warmth of him, the solidity of him.

He's been careful, over the last few weeks, to slow himself down whenever he's with Dymitr. His life is always a breath away from ending, thanks to his role as zemsta, and Dymitr barely knows what he is right now, let alone who he wants to spend time with. And it's far, far too easy for Niko to drink Dymitr down to the dregs.

But this time, when he tries to move away, Dymitr holds on, breathing fast and shallow against Niko's cheek. Too fast. Too shallow.

"Hey," Niko says. "Are you all right?"

Dymitr nods, and Niko studies him for a moment—his eyes are closed, his brow furrowed.

"I don't believe you," Niko says.

Dymitr looks up at him. "It was a difficult day."

Niko thinks of the mint he tasted on Dymitr's breath. "You saw my grandmother."

"The cost of not having the sword is high, but the price Baba Jaga has named for it is higher than I'm willing to pay."

"I see." Niko smooths down Dymitr's T-shirt, but doesn't pull away. "Do you know how many times my mother went to her to ask her to make me into a strzygoń?"

Niko remembers every one. The first time, his mother told him to sit on the top step outside of Baba Jaga's apartment. That's when he tried the mints, popping them in his mouth one after another until his tongue hurt. The next time she dragged him in with her, hoping the sight of him would spark some sense of familial obligation or sympathy. He's not really Baba Jaga's grandchild—more of a great-great-great-grandchild—so he was too far removed from her to make much of an impact. Until later, anyway.

"Four," he says, answering his own question. "Each time before that, my grandmother demanded more than my mother could give. But the fourth time . . . that's when my mother showed up with something of value to bargain with. Understand?"

"I have nothing," Dymitr says. "A passport. A name. A body. That's all."

It takes all of Niko's willpower not to give him a lecherous smile at the mention of having a body.

"What you have is a wealth of knowledge about our enemies that she would otherwise be unable to access," Niko says. "And trust me. There's nothing she wants more than to access that knowledge, no matter what she says."

Dymitr looks thoughtful. He relaxes against the brick and releases the lapels of Niko's jacket.

"You didn't really come here just to return my bow," Dymitr says, and Niko remembers, suddenly, why he's here.

"I leave tomorrow. I just wanted to see you before I go."

"You're leaving? Where are you going?"

Niko tilts his head. Dymitr's ash-brown hair has flopped

over his forehead, skimming his eyebrow. It makes him look younger.

Niko says carefully, "I don't think you really want to know the answer to that question."

"Why wouldn't I—" Dymitr's eyes sharpen with understanding. He looks down. "Oh. You're going on a—mission."

"I prefer to call it 'going hunting,'" Niko says, and he watches Dymitr's face to see his reaction. After all, if it bothers Dymitr that Niko's job is to hunt down Dymitr's old Holy Order friends and exact bloody vengeance, whatever is between them may fizzle out before it even properly catches fire.

Dymitr doesn't meet Niko's eyes.

"It bothers you?" Niko says, stepping back at last.

"It shouldn't."

"But it does."

"That's not your problem, that's mine," Dymitr says curtly.

Niko tastes something bitter in the back of his throat. He rarely thinks of Dymitr as a Knight. Dymitr is someone he wants his hands on, someone he misses when he's alone. Dymitr introduced him to the leszy of Montrose Point Bird Sanctuary like the forest guardian was an old friend, and knows every word of "Bohemian Rhapsody." But if Niko lets his mind drift, he can still see the purple-red that spilled into Dymitr's hands when he picked up his sister's bone sword, the red glint in his eyes, and that question, that question. *Do you know how many of your kind I've killed?* And the answer he gave: *Neither do I.*

"Be careful." Dymitr meets his gaze, then, and he looks painfully sincere, as always. "I don't want anything bad to happen to you."

It should be comforting, maybe, to know that even though Niko's off to murder a Knight, Dymitr is still concerned about him. But the damage is done, the spell of the warm summer night and the buzz of insects broken by memories of past deception.

Still, when Dymitr leans in and touches a featherlight kiss to Niko's cheek, Niko doesn't pull away.

A DESPERATE PLEA

Elza's journey home is long. O'Hare to Zurich, nine-hour flight. Two-hour layover. Zurich to Warsaw, two-hour flight. Warsaw to Gdańsk, one-hour flight. And her mother was waiting for her at the airport, behind the wheel of an old, boxy Škoda. The car's air-conditioning has been broken since they bought it, so the windows are down, and Elza prefers it that way. It means they won't have to talk.

But Marzena is drumming her fingers on the steering wheel, so Elza knows she's agitated. Thanks to the Knights' slow aging, they look like they could be sisters, though Marzena's hair is a deeper brown than Elza's. They both have the high cheekbones and soft, ruddy cheeks of fairy-tale princesses lost in the woods.

Marzena lights up a cigarette once they're outside the city, on the country roads.

"So you ran off, and for what?" Marzena asks, smoke spilling over her lips as she talks. She's wearing sunglasses even though it's cloudy. There's a protective symbol tattooed on the back of each of her fingers. A five-petaled red flower on one. A white eagle from the Polish coat of arms on another.

"I tried to help him." Elza scowls. "Just because he wouldn't accept it doesn't mean it was the wrong thing to do. We travel in pairs for a reason."

"If he wants to get himself killed, let him. The weak should weed themselves out."

It's strange, Elza thinks, that a way of looking at a person can be a habit as surely as biting your nails or cracking your knuckles. When Dymitr was young, he was small for his age, with a soft voice and an even softer heart—he cried whenever mice got caught in the traps, so their father made it his job to set them and empty them. But then he got older, and bigger, and harder, and their grandmother started paying special attention to him, and no one could call him soft after that. But sometimes, it's like her mother forgets that he's no longer a child.

"He's not weak."

"Then he really doesn't need your help anyway, does he?" Marzena flicks her ash out the window. Elza is just considering whether she could fall asleep even with the warm wind blowing through the car's interior when her mother speaks again. "Filip is dead."

She delivers this so casually that Elza hardly notices it, at first. It's just another fact, like what time dinner will be on the table or how warm the weather is. When she finally hears it, she stares at her mother, eyes wide, and all she feels is rage. Filip isn't Marzena's brother, he's their father's brother, but she's still known him for decades. How can she speak of his death so casually, as if it's nothing?

"Pull yourself together," Marzena says, and she tosses the cigarette out the window. Elza watches in the side mirror as it bounces across the road, still lit, and disappears from view.

"How?" Elza asks, and the rage is giving way, now, to something slower and heavier. Filip. Her mentor. Everyone's favorite uncle. He taught her curse words when she was too young for them. He taught her to make pierniki one Christmas, star-shaped and glazed with sugar. He swam with them—Elza and Dymitr and their older brother, Kazik—in the lake at the edge of town, unfazed by the tadpoles. He was deft with a knife.

"Strzyga" is the reply, and at this, Marzena's hands tighten around the steering wheel. Her jaw flexes. All her grief, turned to anger. "I hunted it and killed it already. Your father is cleaning up the aftermath. Filip's body is on its way home."

Tears prick at Elza's eyes, but she can't cry. The last time she cried in front of her mother, Marzena boxed her ear and told her to grow up. That was years ago. Elza breathes deep, until the sharp edges of grief have dulled.

"Good," she says, then. "I hope it died slowly."

"Hear, hear," Marzena says, and she turns on the radio.

Elza drops her bag on the floor of her bedroom and opens the closet door. She didn't bring anything pretty with her to America, just practical clothing that would help her disappear. So she presses her face to a tulle skirt, a silk slip dress, a brocade jacket. They smell like floral perfume, and the textures against her cheek are comforting. She strips off her boots, her jacket, her canvas pants. She puts on pink satin shorts and sits on the edge of her bed.

The door is closed and everyone else is in the kitchen, making plans for the body's arrival. Her cousins just got back from the cemetery, where they picked out a plot to salt it in advance of the burial. Red cabbage is already simmering on the stove, and her aunt is mixing cake batter for yogurt plum cake. Babcia, someone told Marzena, is at the butcher. Elza's job is to get the songbooks out of storage for pustô noc—the empty night.

The empty night is an old ritual, and it only belongs to some members of her family, really. It's Kashubian, and it's her father's side that's Kashubian—Filip's side. Rituals tend to bleed over, regardless, especially when their purpose is to ward off evil spirits. The Holy Order is always interested in warding off evil spirits, so they borrow from every culture, every faith, if it means keeping themselves safe from pollution.

Once the body arrives, they'll put it in the living room on a board, wash it, and wrap its hands in rosary beads. Then the family will gather and pray and sing until daybreak to keep the body safe from dark creatures that want to possess it or transform it. They'll eat and drink and try not to fall asleep. Then they'll carry the body on its plank to the burial plot, and someone will keep watch after it's buried, just to make sure it doesn't rise again.

There's something comforting about knowing what to expect from the next few days, even if Elza doesn't want to see Filip's body, cold and dead, lying on a plank between the chess set and the old record player.

The last time she spoke to Dymitr, he was rude and dismissive, exhorting her to leave him alone as he pursued Baba Jaga. He was with two monsters, a zmora and a strzygoń—a male, which was peculiar—and he kept her from killing one of them. She assumes he needed it to find Baba Jaga, but she doesn't understand why he was pretending to be its ally instead of just taking it hostage. Maybe he was right, though—maybe she shouldn't have gotten involved when she didn't know his plan.

He could have been nicer about it, though. It wasn't like Dymitr to be cruel. But then, he hadn't been acting like himself for months before going to Chicago. Mournful and exhausted. Refusing to draw his sword. Their grandmother kept ordering him to pay penance for his doubt. Hail Marys and kneeling on uncooked peas and God knows what else, in the hope that pain would purge him of whatever ailed him. Apparently it worked, because he came into the kitchen clear-eyed one morning, having proposed an important mission in America that their grandmother had approved.

Elza unlocks her phone and dials his number. She might be angry with him right now, but he loved Filip as much as she did, and he deserves to hear the news. She's not surprised when she gets his voicemail.

"Hello," she says. "I know you're still on your mission, but . . . Filip is dead." Her eyes burn again. This time, with no one to see her, she lets the tears fall. She wipes her nose with the back of her hand so her sniffle won't be audible in the message. "The ritual starts tomorrow night. I don't know how long you're expecting to be gone, but . . ." She chokes a little. "I'd like it if—if you came. Mom is . . . Mom. Everyone's here, and they're—"

She stops. Clears her throat.

"I'd like it if you came," she says again. "But I understand if you can't."

She hangs up before she can say anything even more embarrassing. Then she gets up to pick out a black dress for the funeral.

A PUZZLE SOLVED

There are two of them.

There are always two of them. Knights travel in pairs. Sometimes, when she was still getting visions of them, Ala tried to guess what they were to each other. Siblings. Spouses. Parent and child.

These two are husband and wife. It's obvious in the way they move together, the way they look at each other.

The woman has gray eyes, narrowed in focus, and Ala can tell this event is long past because of the woman's hair, curled and pinned like Marilyn Monroe's even though she's pulling a damn bone sword out of her spine. She yanks it free with a grunt, her hands sticky red, the gray in her eyes now Knight bright. At the corner of her mouth is a cut, like she's been struck.

"Hold her down," the woman says, her voice rough, and she marches toward the man, who has his knee on a zmora's back.

Ala can tell she's a zmora by the way the illusions flicker over her. She gives herself the appearance of a bear, a snake, a fox. The work of a frantic mind and wild illusion powers run amok. In the spaces between them, though, she looks young, her dirty-blond hair tangled over her face, which is pressed to the dirt by the man's palm. He handles her like an animal and maybe that's why she makes herself look like one.

The man's palms are stained red, not with fresh blood, but with the peculiar transformation of a Knight with his bone sword drawn. It's clutched in his left hand, which bears his wedding ring.

"She hit me," the woman says.

"I saw," the man replies.

"I think she should lose the hand she used before she dies," the woman says, and the zmora on the ground screams—in rage or in fear, it's hard for Ala to say.

It's just a dream, Ala says to herself, but it's not just a dream, is it? It's also a memory.

"Just kill me!" the zmora yells. "Just—kill—me!"

The man asks the woman Knight, "Is that really necessary? Lost limbs are so bloody."

The Knights look at each other for a moment, and that seems to be the answer. The man sets aside his bone sword and wrestles one of the zmora's arms free from where he holds them against her back. Then, keeping her pressed to the dirt, he bats aside her attempts to hit him and pins her hand to the ground next to her face.

The first time Ala saw this—when it was provoked by

the bloodline curse that was killing her by inches—she didn't know who either of the Knights were. They were as anonymous as any of the Knights who tormented her.

Now, dreaming of them again, Ala recognizes the woman.

She's Dymitr's grandmother.

Even though she's seen this before, she still expects the woman—Joanna—to position herself over the zmora's arm, bring her sword over her head like an axe, and swing.

That's not what she does.

Instead, she kneels on the ground next to the zmora's head, presses the edge of her bone sword to the zmora's wrist like a bread knife poised over a loaf . . .

And starts to saw.

※

Ala rolls out of bed and stumbles to the bathroom to vomit. She makes it to the sink.

For a long time, sunrise brought her nothing but dread. The first light on the horizon meant the curse would soon latch on to her like a parasite, showing her visions of the Holy Order's violence against all of creaturekind. Monsterkind. Whatever.

These days, daybreak is a relief. She's no longer cursed, but she hasn't forgotten everything the curse made her see. The visions torment her still—but in the form of nightmares.

Ala washes her mouth out, and brushes her teeth. Her

hands are trembling so badly she can barely squeeze out the toothpaste.

She can't take it anymore. This has to stop.

Teeth brushed, she pours herself a cup of coffee and climbs the ladder to the roof to watch the sun come up.

They're not technically allowed on the roof, but the building's landlord is negligent at best, irresponsible at worst, so no one's going to stop them. Dymitr is the one who bought the ladder that's propped up on her back porch. He's also the one who put together the table and chairs that are up there. He didn't mention that he was doing it, just left the finished furniture there for her to find. Dymitr's like that—always willing to make little improvements, even if the tasks are tedious and annoying; always willing to chop something if she's cooking, even if he was already in the middle of something else. The other day she put on a pair of socks to discover he'd mended the holes in the heels with neat stitches. She's not looking forward to the day when he has enough money to move out of her crappy apartment.

Ala sips her coffee, and remembers sitting at the table with her mother in the mornings. Her mother always read the newspaper while Ala did the crossword, and despite often declaring how much she personally *hated* the crossword, she occasionally offered Ala an answer. She was especially good at remembering who won awards—Tonys, Emmys, Grammys, it didn't matter.

The sky is deep pink and she only has half a cup of

coffee left when Dymitr climbs up the ladder himself. He's quicker than a human would be, and he still seems delighted by it, a smug smile on his face as he walks over to the empty chair beside her.

"Good morning," he says. And then, with a look of concern: "What's wrong?"

She hasn't told him about the nightmares. His grandmother—Joanna, who she just watched cut off a zmora's hand, *slowly*—is the one who cursed her family line. And before he knew better, Dymitr killed Ala's aunt, along with countless others. If he knew the curse he helped her break was still tormenting her, but in a new way, he would blame himself. And he'd be, perhaps, a little bit right.

So it's better not to tell him.

"Nothing's wrong," Ala says. "This is just my face."

He frowns. "You smell like—"

"Keep your nose to yourself," she snaps.

It's very annoying, how good his nose is. How he can probably smell the lingering effects of her nightmare, chocolatey and rich.

He looks away, chastened.

"Surprised you're up early," she says. "I saw that Niko returned your bow at some point in the night."

She spotted the guitar case that holds Dymitr's bow and arrow leaning up against the wall in the kitchen.

She's trying to tease him, but his expression is grim.

"He wanted to say goodbye before a . . . hunt."

"Ah."

"He told me to find something of value to Baba Jaga and renegotiate. Something only I could give her."

Ala often feels like she doesn't belong among the not-so-human citizens of Chicago, accustomed as they seem to be to manipulation and subterfuge. She doesn't like to weave around people.

But the image of Dymitr's grandmother with her pinned curls and her bone sword, the zmora's blood splattering her cheeks, is at the very surface of Ala's mind.

Dymitr can't kill his grandmother, as Baba Jaga demanded. But she needs to die.

"Something that belongs to your grandmother, maybe?" Ala says, trying to keep her voice casual. "Where is she now?"

"At home," Dymitr says. "Her house is a kind of . . . home base, for our family. Elza lives there. I . . ." He pauses. "I used to live there, too."

"Does she keep anything important there? A Knight relic or . . ."

Dymitr looks up at her. "I left the book of curses there. The one she used to . . ."

"Curse my family?" Ala asks, with forced brightness. "Yes, I remember."

The image of his grandmother is a stain on her mind. An old lady in a floral blouse, nothing fearsome about her—but when she sat forward with that blue book in her hands, her spine straight and stiff and the fire of a fanatic in her eyes . . .

Yes. She needs to die.

"Would it be valuable to Baba Jaga?" Dymitr says.

Baba Jaga demanded a high price from Dymitr: thirty-three dead Knights, beginning with the one he loves most. There's nothing on Earth that's worth the same. But a book of Knight curses that no one has ever seen before? It might come close.

"If you went back there," Ala says, avoiding the question, "wouldn't your family know what you are right when they see you?"

There's nothing in particular that makes zmoras look different from humans. Eyes too old for their faces, maybe; speech patterns that haven't updated to modern sensibilities. A certain restlessness to their physical forms, like any moment they could shrug on an illusion like an old coat. Lightness, too, and that was what seemed to throw Dymitr off in the weeks following his transformation, his body lacking the same heft. He ran into doorframes and countertops, tripped over his own feet.

But she knows Knights have ways of knowing. Of *seeing*. She just needs him to tell her exactly how. Exactly what.

"She won't look at me that way," Dymitr says firmly.

"How do you know?"

Ala watches the leaves of the nearby catalpa tree flutter

in the breeze. It was covered in white flowers just last week, but a strong wind blew them all into the street overnight, and now they're rotting in the grass and crushed into the sidewalks. Still, it's her favorite tree in the neighborhood, tall with long, crooked branches that attract squirrels.

"It's not something they do casually," he says. "It's an altered state that allows us—" He pauses. Swallows. "That allows *them* . . . to see beyond the surface. Almost as advanced as the one they're in when they draw their swords."

She considers this for a moment.

"Can you still do it?" she asks. "You're a zmora now, but you still have a sword, so you're still part Knight, aren't you?"

He looks into his mug, suddenly tense. "I don't know."

She feels the need to see, the need to know. Just how much of the man she's welcomed into her house, into her *life,* still belongs to the Holy Order? Baba Jaga promised a transformation, but she didn't promise a straightforward one. Maybe Dymitr will always be a Knight. Maybe Ala will either have to make her peace with that . . . or not.

"Try it," she says, and though it's a suggestion, it comes out more like a command.

He looks into his coffee cup for a few seconds longer, and then sets it down on the roof, near his feet. Then he curls one of his hands into a fist, pressing the blunt edge of his fingernails against the meaty part of his hand. She watches him breathe in, and then out, and then he *presses,* cutting into his skin with his fingernails until blood bubbles up around the wounds. She watches in horror as his eyes lift to hers. They gleam bloodred.

She's seen eyes like that so many times. So many Knights standing triumphant over a zmora, a strzyga, a czart, a wraith, a llorona. Their palms purple-red, their swords bone white. Their casual regard of death. A farmer who harvests grain looks at the harvest not with sorrow for the plants he's cut down, but with satisfaction; the Knights are the same way. To them, Ala is . . . a weed. Something to be uprooted and left to rot.

She's so tense her jaw aches. *It's Dymitr,* she tells herself. *He won't hurt you*. But still her heart races as he looks at her, still her body prepares to run as fast as she can.

"It's a shadow," he says, his voice rougher than usual, and grating. "Only instead of following you the way a shadow does, it's inside you. Shifting, like a flame flickering inside a lantern. Like smoke spilling from a thurible."

He opens his fist. The red recedes from his eyes. His hand is still bleeding.

"I frightened you," he says. There's no point in arguing. He can probably taste her terror.

Ala tries to steady herself. She's trembling again.

"I don't know if you know this, but we can't create visions that feature the markers of a Knight," she says. *Breathe,* she tells herself. "The eyes, the hands—they simply don't appear. Many of my kind have tried. An illusion that makes a zmora look like a Knight . . . our magic doesn't allow it."

"Strange," Dymitr says. He's giving her a concerned

look. "All the illusions you can create, and you can't make red eyes?"

Ala shrugs a little.

"Our magic doesn't like your magic—*their* magic," she says. "So while I can't make myself look like a Knight, I think, based on what you just told me . . . I *think* I could still trick a Knight into seeing me as a human instead of a zmora." She pauses. "But in order for you to do that, you would have to be a much more accomplished illusionist than you are now."

She's tried to teach him the art of it, but not every zmora has the same gift for it that she does. He has a sensitive, remarkably well-developed sense of smell, but his illusions are flimsy at best.

"So you do think the book is worth something," Dymitr presses.

"I do," she says, and it's true—the Knights guard their secrets closely, and a book of their curses is a weapon more powerful than she can imagine. "But I think letting any of them lay eyes on you now that you're a zmora is a bad idea."

"It's the only idea I have." There's a note of pleading in his voice. Hardly necessary—she knows the situation he's in. Troubled by pain, and the only hope of respite he's been offered is to kill the woman who raised him. A minor heist does seem like an appealing alternative, even if it's going to be like trying to steal an egg from a pit of vipers.

But there's another solution: Joanna could die by

someone else's hand. That way, Dymitr wouldn't have to do it himself. A small mercy.

"I'll do it instead," she says.

Dymitr is already shaking his head. "No. There's no way you're going anywhere near them—"

"I know what they are. I know what they can do."

"There's knowing and there's knowing," Dymitr says firmly. "They're expecting to see me. They have no reason to suspect that I've *turned into a zmora*—as far as they know, it's impossible. Why would they even check?"

"Of the two of us, which one can make a Knight see whatever they want, you or me?" She gives him a hard look. "Let me help you, at least. You'll be safer with me there."

"Ala. No."

"You don't get to say no like that. Like you're a parent." She feels the barest hint of a tremble in her chin, and she clenches her jaw to control it. "Your grandmother used that book of curses to kill my family, one by one, remember?"

He winces. She feels that twinge of guilt again.

"I remember," he says softly.

"Well, I want it out of their hands more than you do," she says. "So I'm going."

She knows she has him, and he seems to know it, too. He nods.

A FULL BOTTLE

Ala pays for her own plane tickets. Dymitr tried to insist, but it would have depleted all of the money his family gave him for this mission if he'd paid for them both. When he asks her how she can afford it on a bartender's pay, she gives him a level look and says, *Just how old do you think I am, exactly?* He has no idea, of course.

One of the great lies that humanity tells is that time produces wisdom. Oh, Ala will concede that time creates more opportunities for a person to become wise, but it's hardly a guarantee. And for those who don't fear death as much as the average human being, wisdom is even harder to come by. The short mortal lifespan makes the acquisition of wisdom feel urgent, like a survival skill; a long lifespan, by comparison, makes someone feel they have all the time in the world for a slow, contemplative life . . . later.

So Ala doesn't think she seems as old as she is. She certainly doesn't *feel* as old as she is. Her face and body suggest anywhere from twenty-five to thirty; her recollections of recent history, perhaps fifty or sixty. She watched the rise and fall of the boombox, the Walkman, the CD player, the MP3 player, and now the smartphone; she learned to type on a typewriter; she still writes most things in cursive. But in many ways, she's the same age as Dymitr, just finding her footing, uncommitted to anyone but herself.

Her bank account, though, reflects both her age and her dedication to humble living. Her mother was the one who told her that a zmora can't afford to have nothing squirreled away. She might have to flee at a moment's notice, and fleeing is expensive.

When they go through airport security, Ala gets a glimpse of Dymitr's passport. It reads *Dawid Myśliwiec*. At her questioning look, he rolls his eyes and explains that everyone in his family has a legal name and a Knight name. The legal name has to be approved by the government, so it needs to be Polish—but Knights name their children after other Knights from all over the world. She teases him by calling him Dawid all the way to the plane. He refuses to respond.

To get to Gdańsk, they fly a nonsensical route through LaGuardia, at Ala's insistence. There's something she needs to do there. When they land in the new terminal, she grabs Dymitr's wrist and drags him to the fountain in Terminal B. Then she points at an empty chair and tells him to sit and wait. Dymitr's just listening to a voicemail when she walks away from him and faces the fountain.

It's simple in structure, just a wide cylindrical base with a column of water and light falling from the ceiling. It's the light that's remarkable, displaying patterns in the falling water that passersby stop to marvel at, even if they're in an obvious hurry. Right now, the Statue of Liberty glows green in the water column, her torch held high.

Ala tucks her hands into her pockets and takes out something hard and beige. It's an old baby tooth—her mother saved them for her, for just such a purpose. She balances it on her thumbnail and flicks it as hard as she can, so it lands in the middle of the fountain's base—not exactly the kind of fountain you're supposed to throw coins in, but once it touches the metal grate, the tooth disappears, and all of the hair on the back of Ala's neck stands on end.

Standing beside her is a woman. But not *merely* a woman. She has long hair—most wiła do—and her feet are bare, but otherwise she's opted not to look like a figure from an old book of fairy tales. She wears, not a flowing white gown, or a crown of flowers in her hair, but a hot-pink dress that makes her skin look even duller and greener than it would have otherwise. In an attempt to mitigate this, perhaps, she's wearing a lipstick to match the dress—but it's garish on her, and incongruous, like it's painted on a corpse.

Not all women are beautiful by the standard definitions, and not all wiła are, either. This one isn't. There's something froglike about her round eyes and her wide mouth.

"My lady," Ala says, bending her head a little in greeting. The wiła is smaller than Ala is, but much older. It's obvious in the way she appraises Ala, like she's about to correct her posture or scold her for bad manners.

"A zmora," the wiła says, her voice raspy. "How interesting. Are you on a journey, zmora?"

"I am. Back to our homeland."

The wiła snorts. "What reason do you have to go back
there? Everything you need is here."

She gestures to the room around them. No one is paying attention to them, not even Dymitr, who's turned away
from Ala, his phone still pressed to his ear. Everyone is
moving more slowly than usual, too, which is likely due to
the magic created by her tooth donation. It's the price of
speaking to this particular wiła, who's an odd one—living
inside an airport, for one thing; separated from her sisters,
for another.

Wrapped around the circumference of the large room
are restaurants and shops. A Dunkin'. A Hudson Book-
sellers. A Starbucks. She supposes, depending on your pri-
orities, the wiła has a point: everything she needs is here.
A body of water, in the fountain. The lives of mortals, to
observe and occasionally intrude upon. Food, if she de-
sires it. And all the little debts and sacrifices that build
on each other day by day—taking an earlier flight to see
a loved one sooner, or giving up a seat so the plane can
leave on time, or just the thankless labors of the airport
employees who frequent this place—which create the po-
tential for strong magic, if someone knows how to make
use of them.

"Is that man your friend?" the wiła asks. When Ala
nods, she says, "I had friends, once." She sounds wistful.

"We used to dance and sing together in the river. Then mortals came and built a dam, and the river dried up, and we had to scatter. I don't know where my friends are now. I gave up looking for them long ago."

"I'm sorry, my lady," Ala says.

The light from the fountain is reflected in the wiła's dark, round eyes.

"The world always changes," the wiła says. "For now, it changes to exclude us. Someday it may change to suit us once more. But not yet." She looks at the fountain again. "You've come to ask me for something, but I only help warriors, and most zmoras I have met can't claim to be warriors. Are you an exception?"

She looks at Dymitr, who still has a phone pressed to his ear, and says, "I'm going to kill a Knight."

The wiła raises her thin eyebrows. "And you believe you can accomplish this?"

"I'm not an experienced killer," Ala says. "But I'm excellent at illusions. I have a plan to get close to her. I just need your help for the last part of it."

"Then you'd better ask, zmora. Your tooth won't buy us much more time."

"I don't speak the language, where I'm going," Ala admits. It's not exactly shameful, but it makes her feel sheepish, like it's some personal failure. As if she doesn't deserve to claim their mother country if she can't speak its language . . . even though it wasn't her choice, not to be taught.

"To purchase fluency would be costly indeed."

"I don't need it to be permanent. Only while I'm visiting."

Ala is wary of her own request, wary of its cost. She could have gone to a lesser witch for something like this, but a lesser witch might give her the ability to speak Polish, but only in someone else's voice, or they might have made her forget English in the process, or she could speak Polish, but only at night or only at the full moon. Everyone knows that if you want something to do with the voice, you go to a wiła. She'll do it properly.

"For as long as you speak our mother tongue, you will lose the ability to speak for twice that time upon your return," the wiła says, after a moment. "If you stay for a day, you'll give me your voice for two days. If you stay for a week, you'll give me your voice for two weeks. Understand?"

"Yes, my lady." Ala doesn't love the idea of losing her voice for that long, but of all the bargains she could have made, it seems the most straightforward she could have hoped for. Because wiła only help warriors, they tend to be more up front about the costs of their magic. If they're going to turn on you, they do it right away, before the bargaining even begins.

The wiła reaches into the pocket of her puffy skirt, and takes out a crystal bottle, small enough to fit in her palm. She takes the stopper out of it, and offers it to Ala.

"Whisper your name into this bottle," she says. "And it will be done."

Ala takes the bottle and holds it up to her lips. *"Aleksja Dryja,"* she whispers, and then the wiła takes it and stoppers it. For a moment, Ala thinks, *Is that all?* She's not good at sensing magic, as a general rule. But then she smells petrichor, and the fountain in front of her starts to look . . . strange. Strings of water pull away from the column like hair blowing in a strong wind. They stretch toward her and then wrap around her, not quite touching her, but distorting her vision. It's like trying to see through a waterfall.

She looks at the wiła through the curtain of water, and notices for the first time that her bare feet don't seem to be touching the tile. She's floating a half inch above the ground.

Ala can tell the moment the time-slowing magic runs out, because all the water collapses against her at once, soaking her from head to toe. She splutters, water running into her eyes and ears and mouth. Everyone around her stares at her like they're waiting for an explanation, but Ala doesn't offer one. She just walks back over to Dymitr, running a hand over the back of her neck to keep a drop of water from rolling down her spine.

He's staring into the middle distance, his phone still in hand. When she touches his shoulder, he startles a little, and blinks at her.

"What happened?" she asks him.

"Why are you *wet*?" he replies.

"Say something in Polish and I'll tell you."

"Um . . . why are you wet?" he asks again, and for a moment she thinks he just said it again in English, before her lagging mind processes the sound of the words he spoke.

"I understood that." She grins. "Thanks to the wiła who lives in the fountain. It's only temporary."

She can feel her mouth moving in unfamiliar ways over the consonants, but she can no longer remember the feeling of not understanding them. It's as if this is knowledge she's had all her life.

Dymitr is staring. "You sound different. Your voice is . . . lower."

"So is yours." And it's interesting to hear him in his own language, how much deeper and flatter he sounds. More authoritative than in English, where he's more tentative, maybe, or gentler. And maybe it's because the languages define a shift in him, with Polish the language of his Knighthood and English the language of his transformation.

She looks at the phone in his hand, clutched so tight his knuckles are white.

"What happened?" she asks again.

"My sister left me a message. Our uncle is dead." His matter-of-factness is a little startling to Ala, though not surprising. Her mother was like that, too, in her declarations.

Why dress it up? Better to just say it, she often said, when Ala scolded her for insensitivity.

But she's gotten to know Dymitr over the last few weeks, and while there are many shades to his grief, the darkest one is when he shows no emotion at all.

"I'm sorry," she says.

"He was a Knight."

"I'm not sorry for him; I'm sorry for you." She touches Dymitr's arm, lightly. He's wearing a black denim jacket from the resale shop. When he got it, there was a patch on the shoulder from a national park, but he picked out the stitches to remove it, and now there's just a dark circle where it used to be. "Your sister wants you to go to the funeral?"

"Yes." Dymitr doesn't quite meet her eyes. "Well, that too. She wants me to come to the house for the pre-funeral rituals with everyone."

"With everyone?"

"Cousins. Aunts and uncles. My brother and parents. Everyone."

Ala's chest tightens. The plan was to go to Dymitr's near-empty house to steal the book—where they would be alone, or nearly alone, with his grandmother. Now the house will be stuffed to the brim with Knights?

She'll have no chance. No chance at all, to rid the world— and herself—of this woman who haunts her dreams. To spare Dymitr the pain of having to do it himself, or else surrender to madness.

"We should find out if they can change our tickets," she says. "How long does the funeral last? We could maybe go next week—"

"What do you mean?" Dymitr says. "I'm still going. It will give me a good excuse to show up there, and the chaos will make it easier to get the book. They'll be too busy to pay close attention to me."

"You can't possibly be considering this," Ala says. "You have to at least wait until the funeral, when the house is empty. Don't give them a chance to see you like this."

"I know you're worried. But trust me, it will be fine. They have no reason to suspect anything of me. And my uncle . . ." He slides his phone into his pocket, and looks down. "My uncle was kind to me. I'd like to mourn him properly."

There's just a slight wavering—in his voice, in his lower lip. Then he picks up his bag.

She wants to argue with him. No matter how confident he is that his family won't suspect him, she's still unnerved by the thought of him walking into that house like nothing has changed. Can't they tell that he's not one of them?

She can. She has from the start.

But he's right—they have no reason to suspect that he's changed. Not when they believe change is impossible.

She'll just have to find an opportunity to get his grandmother alone. Maybe on her way to the funeral, maybe the day after, while she sleeps, maybe—

He says, "Come on, I want to see if the shop has Baked

Lay's," and she decides to save the brainstorming for another time.

Instead, she makes a face. "The entire array of American snack foods is in front of you, and you're on a quest for *Baked Lay's*? They taste like almost nothing."

"No, they taste both salty and bland," he says. "All the comfort of a saltine cracker but with the satisfying snap of a chip."

"Are the Lay's people paying you to say this? Blink twice if you're being blackmailed."

Dymitr just grins, and leads the way to the store.

Ala ignores the gnawing in her stomach. It feels a lot like dread.

A CHANCE ENCOUNTER

The red tile roofs are how he knows he's home. The little stucco houses clustered together with fields all around. The wrought-iron gates and metal fences. Narrow roads with village dogs running along them. Sagging sheds of corrugated metal or rotting wood.

Ala sleeps in the passenger seat as he drives the rental car, which smells like old cigarettes and whatever cleaner they used to get that cigarette smell out, like stale french fries and floral perfume and windshield wiper fluid. He stops at a gas station and picks up a packet of paluszki. He has one between his teeth like a cigarette when Ala wakes.

"How long before Mieczyk?" she asks.

The town of Mieczyk is nestled in the trees southwest of Gdańsk. It's big enough to disappear in, so it's big enough that mortals and not-so-mortals alike live alongside each other. A half hour north of it is a village, small and overlooked, where Dymitr's family lives. Dymitr spent most of his life going back and forth between Mieczyk and the village, close enough to the forest to disappear there when he needed to. And he often needed to, thanks to the relentless teasing of his cousins and brother.

Some people in Mieczyk know what Knights are and what they fight. Some don't. His grandmother always knew which people were which.

"Twenty minutes," he says, because even though the town's not far from them, they need to drive all the way around it to get to the hotel without passing through his family's village.

He turns onto packed-dirt roads and they drive through fields of overgrown grass and stretches of tall trees with slim trunks. Sunlight dapples the ground in front of them. He opens the window to breathe in the smell of dirt baking in the sun. He feels a kind of pressure against the right side of his head, like a headache is building.

"Do you have any other siblings?" Ala asks.

"A brother. Kazimierz," he says. "Or Kazik, as we call him."

She must hear something in his voice, because she grins. "You don't like him."

"He was fine when we were younger. But when he got too old to play with us, he became insufferable." He glances at her. "As if you're ever too old for a cool fort in the woods."

Ala laughs, and says, "Kazik, Elza, and Dymitr. An interesting assortment of names."

"We're named for well-known Knights. Kazik's namesake was Polish—one of our ancestors—and killed by a wraith. Elza's was from a Latvian family, and she was killed by a vilkač—like a werewolf. Mine was Russian. Killed by a strzyga."

"So they'd find your choice of romantic partner . . . especially galling?"

Dymitr's mouth curls into something that he's sure looks like a smile, even if it doesn't feel like one. "That's the least of my worries, at this point."

Ala nods, and rubs her temple with her fingertips. "The air feels weird here."

Dymitr doesn't answer for a moment. He listens to the wind shuddering through the car. He smells something like horseradish in the air; likely from garlic mustard plants growing nearby. They pass a field dotted with gladiolus, the flower that gives the town its name.

Eventually he says, "We're driving around the place where my family lives. So I think what you're feeling is their magic."

"It doesn't feel like magic."

"The Holy Order's magic comes from pain. The pain is a sacrifice, so it creates space for magic, like any other sacrifice—but it's different. It feels different."

He's been able to sense it since he split his soul to become a Knight. But he didn't feel this way about it before. Before, coming home felt like stepping into a quiet room. Like a museum or a library. It felt sacred. But now, the way it presses against him . . . it's like something that was alive in the air, something that danced around him, is now dead. The silence is stifling.

He takes a strange, circuitous route to the hotel, and he's relieved when that pressure, that silence, lets up again. The hotel is at the end of a dirt road, surrounded on three sides by fields. There's a pile of rubble next to the parking lot—an abandoned construction site—but the hotel itself looks nice enough. It's a white building in the Tudor style, with a red roof. It looks more like a large house than a hotel, but the reviews were good and the rooms were cheap.

A bored-looking twentysomething checks them in, and they set their bags down in a worn-out room with bright orange carpeting. There are two twin beds with thin mattresses inside it, but the bathroom is clean and there's an air-conditioning unit on the wall, so they won't be too hot when they sleep. Dymitr takes the bed closer to the door, and he falls into an uneasy sleep while Ala takes a shower.

He dreams about Ala's cousin, Lena. The last zmora he killed—or at least, the last zmora he didn't stop his sister from killing.

She looked like Ala—or like a version of Ala that could have existed in another world. She wore black eyeliner with sharp wings, and tight black clothing no matter the weather. By the time he arrived, she was already dying, a short sword sticking out of her belly. Elza had gone ahead of him to the house. Lena's father wasn't there—probably draining his second beer while Knights killed his daughter, at his request.

But in the dream, Lena is sitting at the table when he arrives, her father across from her. He's slumped on the white lace tablecloth—sleeping or dead, it's hard for Dymitr to say. Lena is writing a message on a yellow legal pad, but she's using a quill and red ink. She doesn't greet him, but she reaches out to stick the quill into her father's mouth, and it comes away red, which is how he recognizes the ink as blood.

It's a mundane scene, though grotesque, but Dymitr can't look away from it, and it fills him with such dread he can hardly stand it. That dread follows him to the waking world, where Ala is stepping through the door, her short hair mostly dry. He stares up at her for a moment, still half-convinced she's another Lena. The other half, the half that still feels guilty for Lena's death, knows that can't be true.

"You're afraid," she says, and she sniffs the air, like she's trying to determine exactly what kind of fear he's feeling.

"Bad dream," he manages to reply. "You went out?"

She's carrying a long, thin box, too big to hold a necklace but too small for anything else he can think of. She lifts the lid and shows him a knife with a sturdy handle.

"There are zmoras here, too. Klara gave me a name," she says. "They were helpful."

Dymitr's stomach turns. "And what do you intend to do with a knife?"

"We're close to a lot of Knights. I'm not going to stay here unarmed." She doesn't quite meet his eyes. "What's our plan?"

"We'll drive out to their house at dusk," he says, "and then . . . I have an idea. It'll keep you out of harm's way."

"Let me guess: it puts you directly into harm's way, instead."

Dymitr holds up his hands in surrender. "It allows us both to keep the other safe. Okay? I just need to work out some of the details."

She doesn't look convinced. In fact, he catches a whiff of powdered-sugar sweetness—she's nervous. Well, of course she's nervous. But there's something different about this scent. He closes his eyes as he breathes it in. It's darker than pure anticipation. Deeper.

He's not a fool. He knows Ala is struggling with something. She smells like terror every morning, and apprehension at bedtime. But if she doesn't trust him enough to talk to him about it, it's not his place to ask.

She sighs, and looks at the wall clock. "Can we get caffeine?"

"I know a place."

Dymitr trips into the bathroom to stick his head under the faucet.

The first time Dymitr went to Basia's Cafe was after scouting.

Every prospective Knight had a mentor. On the day of the winter solstice, the darkest night of the year, the family gathered and all the young people sat in the kitchen, and if they'd been chosen to begin their Knight education, they were called into the living room to find out who had selected them. Dymitr's father, Łukasz, chose his older brother when he was just ten years old, claiming he was maturing fast. Elza, despite being younger than Dymitr, came a few years later, picked by their uncle Filip. And Dymitr kept sitting in the kitchen with all the cousins far younger than he was—doomed, he thought, to learn to cook and never to fight.

That was before he knew that his grandmother had chosen him years before, when he was still just a child. She had her reasons for delaying in telling him. *I wanted to make you patient,* she said to him once, almost as an apology. *I wanted to test your resolve.* She had a way of making suffering feel almost like heroism.

For the first few years of his apprenticeship to her, she took him out to the countryside to scout. Scouting was as important as fighting, according to his grandmother. She taught him simple things first, like tracking. He could identify a particular set of boot prints on a forest trail; he could find the places where they broke sticks or bent grass with their movements. Then, because monsters had folded themselves into the modern world, she taught him how to find people using modern means. *Everyone leaves a trail, my boy.*

He had just located a strzyga for her, finding first the alias she was using and the apartment where she was staying, and then identifying her boot prints in a nearby field. His grandmother ordered him to stay put while she took care of the rest. She returned fifteen minutes later with blood under her fingernails and a smile on her face, and she took him to Basia's to celebrate. While she washed her hands in the cafe's bathroom, Dymitr looked over the menu and chose a coffee and a pastry, rewards for a job well done.

Now, as he walks toward the cafe with Ala, he thinks there was another reason his grandmother delayed his education: she wanted him to be starved for approval and desperate to please. She believed it would make him a better student. And she was right.

"All right, I can't take it anymore," Ala says, after they've been walking for ten minutes. They're passing an Orange store with rows of phone cases hanging on the wall, and a discount supermarket with a big ladybug on the sign. She turns to him, a little unsteady on the cobblestones.

"What are you afraid of, exactly?" she says to him. "We're not likely to run into your family here, are we?"

"It's not that."

"Then what is it? You smell like a patisserie. Don't get me wrong, I don't mind having the consistent food source—"

"Everything is the same," Dymitr says, cutting her off mid-sentence. He gestures vaguely to the street ahead of them. "The stores, the streets. All the same as when I was . . ." *As when I thought you weren't a person,* he thinks. *As when I thought it was my duty to kill you.* "But nothing's the same. The more I remember, the more I realize that every memory I have here is a horror, even the good ones."

It feels like finding a spot on an apple, he thinks. You hope that you can just slice it away and still eat the rest of the fruit. But then you discover the flesh is brown all the way to the wormy core.

"I'm afraid of what I'm going to find here," he says.

Ala's hand twitches, like she's going to reach for him, and then she seems to think better of it. She's not a demonstrative person, and he prefers it that way. If she tried to offer comfort, it would crush him. Better, then, to just see her nod, and to fall into step beside her as they cross the street.

Basia's Cafe is just around the bend. He sees the familiar blue letters fixed to the side of the building, a little crooked. The grid of blue-glass windows. And the small blue tables in front where he used to sit with his grandmother.

He half expects to see her there, sipping her espresso, her eyes narrowed at the passersby because she's nearsighted but never wants to wear her glasses.

Instead, though, he sees a man. He has dark hair and light brown skin and despite the cloud cover, he's wearing a pair of sunglasses. When he lifts his coffee cup to his lips, Dymitr sees that his fingernails are black.

Nikodem Kostka is sitting at Basia's Cafe.

A BARGAIN STRUCK

Anywhere there are Knights, Niko knows, there are informants. After centuries of being hunted, most quasi-mortals—as Ala would call them—are pretty good at evading the Holy Order. So even the most rigid Knight knows they need a little bit of hypocrisy to keep the whole operation running. In other words, they need help from the quasi-mortals themselves. The vulnerable and the desperate will go to great lengths to save their own skin . . . or the skin of their loved ones.

Niko is sympathetic, to a point. He's never been in a position to make that kind of choice. He's pretty sure he knows what he would do if he was—or what he wouldn't do—but then, strzygas are stronger and fiercer than most, and it's harder for them to hide what they are, what with the fingernails and the owl eyes, so they've had to learn to be smart, too.

It's the harmless ones who have more limited options. Czarts. Zmoras. Kikimoras. Banshees. Anyone who isn't strong enough to rely on force. If they're clever, they don't have to turn on their own people to protect themselves . . . but not everyone is born clever.

So he's careful of everyone he passes when he's hunting, even the ones he's pretty sure aren't human.

He has a contact in the city nearest to his hunting ground—the brother of a zmora Feliks avenged a few years back—who points him toward the wieszczy.

A known traitor, but perhaps a sympathetic one, given the circumstances. The wieszczy lives in a town with cobblestone streets and an old church at its center. The church is all red: red brick with a terracotta tile roof, red trim around its heavy wooden doors. The bell tower is the tallest point for miles. And tucked away in an alley, still close enough to be in the bell tower's shadow, is a little apartment where the wieszczy lives.

Niko goes to its door at dusk, still wearing his sunglasses. It's too warm to get away with wearing gloves at this time of year, so he painted his fingernails black, instead. He doesn't like nail polish much, but his kind don't get to pick the color of their talons, so to speak, and his are dark, like the face of the owl he wears when he transforms. He raises his fist and knocks on the apartment door.

There aren't many creatures who begin their lives as human, but the wieszczy is one. Born with cauls on their heads. Born with pink cheeks and an eager, busy nature. Born with spots of blood under their fingernails. Or so the legends say.

There aren't many of them, so Niko doesn't know fact

from fiction. He only knows that after they die, they rise again with a craving for human flesh, even if it's their own. And they remain that way, dead but not dead, hungry but not sated, until they eat enough of their own bodies to crumble into dust, or until someone kills them. *The most pitiful of all the pitiful creatures that walk the earth,* his mother used to say, *and they don't deserve our scorn.*

The woman who answers the door is shrouded in darkness. She wears all black, her garments overlarge, so they cover her hands and any shape she has. She looks up at him through a curtain of dark hair. What little of her skin he can see is pale and sickly as a frog's belly.

"Can I help you?" she asks him—in Polish, of course, and he understands it well, even though his accent is—as Dymitr says—hard on the ears.

He takes off his sunglasses. His eyes are just a little too orange to be normal—just enough for attentive humans to comment on when he's checking out at the grocery store. And just enough for the wieszczy to understand, not what he is exactly, but that he's something other than human.

"What do you want?" she asks, her tone harsh. She's starting to shut the door, even as she asks the question.

Niko puts his foot in the doorjamb, and leans closer.

"I mean you no harm," he says, "but I won't let you push me out, either. Not until I've spoken to you."

The wieszczy doesn't quite meet his eyes. She steps away from the door, though, and he slips inside the apartment.

The door leads right into the kitchen, where there are

dishes piled high in the sink and stacks of newspapers covering the little table. Empty paper bags smeared with fruit jam litter the countertop along with cartons of maślanka. All the windows are covered with cardboard. It smells like sour milk.

The wieszczy fidgets and shifts. There's a kettle of water on the stove with steam pouring from its spout. She turns the burner off. As her hand emerges from beneath the drape of her sleeve, he sees she only has three fingers—thumb, index, and middle. For a moment he wonders how she lost them, and then he thinks of her clawing her way out of the grave, desperately hungry for flesh no matter whose it is, and his mouth goes dry.

"Didn't think I'd ever see a strzygoń in this town again," she says. She speaks with a lisp.

"I'm only visiting."

"*Visiting.*" She laughs. "Flirting with death is what you're doing. Do you know who lives near here?"

"I'm well aware." Niko hooks his foot around a chair leg and tugs it back from the table, then sits, though he wasn't invited to.

The wieszczy hooks two fingers around the handle of a cabinet door and takes down a box of cherry tea. She fumbles with the box for a while before she gets a bag out of it. She drops the bag in a mug waiting on the counter. Her other hand stays hidden in her sleeve.

"Then what is the purpose of your visit?"

"I was sent here as part of my vengeance oath."

At that, her hands falter. She leans into the counter, her shoulders bunching up around her ears.

"Do it, then," she snaps.

She's braced in anticipation of a blow, he realizes. She expects him to kill her.

A zemsta's job must have been easier in the time when you could carry weapons without causing alarm, Niko thinks. As it is, he has a knife hidden in his boot and another one strapped to his forearm, which means he has to wear long sleeves no matter how warm it is. Not ideal, for being so close to the Holy Order he can practically taste their magic in the air, but he can't really walk around town with a sword at his hip.

"I'm not taking vengeance against *you*," he says. "But I did come for your help."

She relaxes by a fraction, and pours water over the tea bag. Then she turns toward him. The light from the stove shines across her scarred cheek, and he realizes why she has a lisp—her lower lip is gone, and only scar tissue remains.

"I'm hunting one of them," Niko says. "Someone who's notoriously difficult to pin down, but they're here, now, for a funeral. Along with . . . quite a few others."

He's still certain that Lidia sent him here to die, but she doesn't know Niko. He's cleverer than his predecessor, and he knows that if he's going to hold his own against the Razor, he'll need help, and he'll need to use the circumstances—a house full of Knights, all gathered to put one of their number into the ground—to his advantage.

"The bees are swarming the hive, and you want to stick your hand in it?" The wieszczy laughs, and sips her cherry tea. The red liquid dribbles down her chin like blood. She doesn't bother to wipe it away. "You must be new."

"I'm not, as a matter of fact." Niko is getting annoyed. "Anyway, it's not your concern, whether I'm likely to succeed or not. You're either going to do what I ask, or you're not, regardless of the outcome."

"And why would I consider doing what you ask?"

"Because of the *czart,* Maja," Niko says harshly, and when he speaks her name the air seems to crackle as if charged with electricity. Niko closes his eyes, and takes a deep breath. There's no sense in wasting magic—not here, not now.

But maybe it wasn't a waste, because it seems to remind the wieszczy exactly who and what he is. Not just a strzygoń, but someone whose oath provides him with a constant flow of magic. The sacrifice of his safety, his ambitions, his dreams—it's created a debt that can never be repaid. When he opens his eyes, the wieszczy is holding the teacup in both mangled hands, looking stricken.

"I didn't mean to—" she says, and her breath catches.

"Of course not," Niko says, his voice soft and soothing. "You only meant to get the czart killed, didn't you? And no one cares about a czart, do they? It's not your fault he had friends with him when the Knight came calling. It's not your fault six people died when you only intended one."

The wieszczy bows over the mug of tea, pulling into herself like a bug curling up to die.

"I was human, once," she says.

"So was I." Niko leans back in his chair. "Ask me how many creatures I got killed when I was still mortal."

"Mortal," she scoffs. "How can a strzygoń be born human?"

"My long life was bought at a terrible price. Though perhaps not as terrible a price as the six lives your survival cost."

The wieszczy's eyes are dark. They remind him of rain puddles in moonlight, just a sheen of light on black pavement. Her expression is neutral, as if their discussion means nothing to her, but guilt is just anger and shame intermingling, so he can feel it as surely as he felt the prickle of her anger before. He has more sympathy toward her than he lets on. It's hard not to. Either she lived a normal human life, if her parents didn't know what signs to look for in their newborn, or she lived a life under the shadow of dread, if they did. To be a wieszczy is to know all your life that after the horror of death, there will be a new horror: a mouthful of grave dirt, a taste for flesh, and an endless un-life.

It amazes him still, how she was so desperate to preserve even that half life, that horror life, that she offered up someone else's suffering and destruction. No matter what someone is, the living still want to live, most of the time.

"What do you want me to do?" she says.

"A simple task," he answers. "The Holy Order are performing a ritual to ward off evil spirits. To ensure that their lost brother doesn't come back as something else." He smiles a little. "I believe they are mainly concerned that he'll wake as—"

"A wieszczy," the wieszczy says testily. "Yes. This ritual comes from *my* people, after all."

"So I've heard. My request, therefore, is that you let them catch sight of you at the cemetery. They'll scatter to search for you. And I'll be able to corner my quarry."

"You're so sure you can get them alone?"

"I know her patterns," Niko says. "And once she sees me, well. I'm not exactly difficult to identify as a strzygoń."

"Bad luck for you." The wieszczy's upper lip curls, revealing too much tooth. Her incisors are pointed, a little jagged at the ends. Good for rending flesh, he supposes.

"I get by," he says.

"If I do this, I'll have to flee," the wieszczy says. "I can't live here anymore."

"Then I suppose it's up to you to decide how much you love this place and the life you've made here," Niko says, shrugging. "If you help me, you'll no longer be shunned by my people. You can seek refuge with them in the city, if you like. And you will attain some small amount of redemption for what you did. Only you can say how much that's worth to you."

Niko watches her for a moment. He knows of magic that can tug her in one direction or another, but he doesn't think he'll need it here. He thinks she'll agree all on her own.

When she doesn't respond for a few long seconds, he stands, and pushes his chair in. A newspaper slides off the table and onto the dirty tile floor. The wieszczy sets her mug down on the counter, still mostly full of dark red tea. He nods to her, and makes his way to the door.

"I'll do it," she says, when he turns the knob.

He smiles to himself.

It takes fifteen minutes of walking to get rid of the smell of old milk from his nose, and even then, he can't quite lose it. He steps into a cafe to breathe in the scent of coffee and orders a cappuccino, which he drinks at the blue table outside, his sunglasses still on though it's far too dark for that now.

He's just considering whether he wants to stick his finger into the cup to get the last bits of foam from the bottom when he looks up . . . and sees Dymitr walking down the street.

Niko stops, the cup still in hand. Dymitr stops. Beside him, Ala stops.

For a moment, they're all still. Niko's mind is flooded

with questions. But he can't ask any of them, not here, not in full view of the street. He stands, leaving his coffee cup behind, and nods toward the nearest side street. It's almost as tight as an alley, hemmed in on either side by white stucco buildings with rust-colored metal fences. Somewhere nearby, a dog is barking.

Niko takes off his sunglasses and hooks them over his shirt collar. Dymitr is there in front of him, with the same air of mild neglect that he usually has, his clothes creased and his hair disheveled. As ever, Niko has the urge to smooth down his edges and piece him back together. But he keeps his hands to himself.

Ala lingers a few steps behind him, looking uncertain. Uneven.

"What are you doing here?" Dymitr says quietly, in English. Demands, really, because there's urgency in his voice, in his eyes.

"What are *you* doing here?" Niko says. "Did you guys follow me here, or something?"

"Oh, come on," Ala says, arms folded. "You both know why the other is here."

And he does, doesn't he? Because why would Dymitr be here, in this little town in northwest Poland . . . unless he was from here?

"Myśliwiec," Niko says. "Your name is Dymitr Myśliwiec."

People are named for so many things—where they're from, or some paternal name, or some quirk of their appearance, like red hair or always wearing green. But they're also named for their trade, and *Myśliwiec* means *hunter*. It's almost funny. Niko almost laughs.

He's here to kill a member of Dymitr's family.

"Yes," Dymitr says softly. And then: "Who is your . . . quarry?"

Niko meets Ala's eyes, as if she can offer him some guidance—but he knows there's none to be had. They're breaking new ground here. A real fucked-up Romeo and Juliet scenario, only the Capulets didn't hunt down and brutally murder every single Montague they could get their hands on.

Niko says, "Again, I don't think you really want to know the answer to that question."

It's after sunset now, and everything has a blue tint to it, even the faultless gray of Dymitr's eyes. A group of teenagers walks along the main street, talking too loud; a bell rings; a car drives by.

"I'm gonna . . . go be the lookout," Ala says, stepping away from them. "I'll let you know if anyone's coming."

She walks to the end of the street and faces away from them.

A tingle creeps across Niko's shoulders, and it's the feeling of Dymitr's frustration. If it wasn't directed at him, he would enjoy it more.

"Tell me," Dymitr says.

"I can't do that. If it turns out to be someone you care about . . ."

The tingling sensation turns into something deeper, heavier. It prickles in Niko's bones. Goose bumps rise up on his arms; he shivers, even as Dymitr puts a finger on his chest and pushes him—carefully, but not quite gently—up against the metal fence behind him.

Niko stares down at him, bewitched for a moment.

"Tell me," Dymitr says, and now it sounds like he's begging.

Niko says quietly, "Do you understand that if I tell you who it is and you warn them, you could get me killed?"

Dymitr closes his eyes. His hand presses flat to Niko's chest. "I won't warn them. I would never put you at risk like that."

Niko believes him, even though that's absurd. He's absurd.

"The locals call her 'the Razor,'" Niko says. Even his fluent tongue tripped over the word in Polish—brzytwa. Not all Knights are well known; this one's address fell immediately from the mouths of the local strzygas, like a curse.

Dymitr laughs, and turns away, his hand coming up to cover his mouth. He paces into the middle of the street, where weeds have begun growing between the cobblestones.

Niko says, "You know her, I take it."

"Whoever gave you this mission wants you dead," Dymitr says. "You should leave. Go home, refuse this, don't get anywhere near her—"

"That's not how it works."

"I don't care how it works." Dymitr turns on him, crowds him up against the fence again. "If you try to do this, you'll die."

Niko tries on a half smile. "Why, Dymitr. Should I be *offended* that you think so little of me?"

Dymitr doesn't look amused. "You should be afraid of Marzena Myśliwiec."

"You told me, once, that you didn't keep track of how many of my kind you'd killed," Niko says, cold now. "Well, I haven't kept track of how many of yours I've killed, either. You shouldn't underestimate me just because you've had your tongue in my mouth."

Dymitr flinches a little. "I'm not underestimating you. I'm correctly estimating her."

Niko did his research before he came here. He knows the Razor is known for the ease with which she uses magic, and the relentless, methodical way she approaches her kills. No recklessness for Marzena Myśliwiec; she's like a machine. He can't imagine her with a family. He can't imagine she was ever very kind to the one she has.

So his voice is softer when he asks Dymitr, "Who is she to you?"

"My mother."

Niko receives the word like a blow. This is too much Shakespearean tragedy for him.

"Your *mother* is the fucking *Razor*?" Niko says. "God, how did you turn out so . . . *normal*?"

Dymitr's eyes are too bright. "I can't do this."

"I have to do my job. She's a killer, Dymitr."

"She's my mother," Dymitr says again, fiercer this time. "I love her. I will always love her. No matter what happens here, I'll lose. If she dies— If you die—"

"I am not going to die."

"Then you're going to be the one who kills my mother," Dymitr says. "And I'll never be able to look at you again. Do you understand that?"

A tear spills down his cheek and he wipes it away, forcefully, with the heel of his hand. Niko's chest aches.

"Shh." Niko covers Dymitr's hands—currently knitted in his hair—with his own. "Yes, yes, I understand."

He runs his fingers over Dymitr's knuckles, and then tugs him closer, so Dymitr's head touches his chest. He's trembling.

It's too much to ask of any heart, Niko thinks. To turn so fully against the ones you love, even once you've realized what they really are. It's just too much.

Dymitr pulls away, red-eyed and disheveled as ever. He looks up at Niko.

"She keeps a knife in her left boot," Dymitr says. Then his face contorts, as if he's in pain, and he walks away from Niko so fast he's almost running—past Ala, past the cafe, and into the night.

A FAMILY REUNION

Elza is there when they carry Filip's body in. There's a cousin at each shoulder, and her brother Kazik at the feet. They carry it through the house and into the living room, where they set it down on a long board that someone brought in from the garden shed for just this purpose. Filip isn't the first person who's died from that part of the family, and he won't be the last.

Her mother is the one who killed the strzyga that killed Filip, but her father is the one who went to Germany to pick up all the pieces and clean things up. He was always better at that than Marzena, who would have been arrested a dozen times over if not for him.

Her father cast preservation magic over the body before sending it back. He must have given some real pain to ensure the magic was strong enough to keep the body from decomposing, because Filip looks like he could be sleeping. His skin is powder white, but his eyes are closed and his hands, stained with old blood, are folded over the hilt of his bone sword.

The killing blow is in his throat. The strzyga's claw, maybe, or its beak. The wound is wrapped in gauze, so Elza can't see it.

Her grandmother walks into the living room, and everyone stiffens all at once. She surveys the body. Filip wasn't related to her by blood, but he and his brother—Elza's father—were a package deal, promised to marry two of Joanna's daughters when they came of age. So her grandmother has known—had known—Filip since he was a child. He was like one of her own sons.

Yet there's no feeling in her voice when she says, "Krystyna and I will wash him. Kazik, cover all the mirrors. Elza, set the clocks. He died at five after ten."

It's all so pointless, Elza thinks, as she walks to the wall clock to turn the hands. Covering mirrors and opening windows to clear the way for his soul. Stopping the clocks at Filip's time of death, to tell him that his time is ended. But she does it, winding the clock back so its hands point at the ten and the one. She moves into the kitchen to change the clock on the microwave, feeling like a ghost.

She wanders through the house in pursuit of other clocks, and behind her she can hear Krystyna, the new widow, murmuring to the body as she tells it what she's doing. *We'll start with your neck, okay? Let me just get this gauze off.* Elza wonders if she should set all of the watches to 10:05, too, or if that's too much. She checks her phone to see if Dymitr called; he hasn't.

Her cousin Teresa is in the kitchen making cabbage

rolls with her son André—his Knight name. Elza can hear him complaining about working in the kitchen like he's not a proper Knight. "Well, you aren't," Teresa says sharply. "So until you do the ritual, you will help your mother!"

Elza sees her mother standing in the doorway to the living room, watching as Krystyna and her own mother—Joanna, fearsome matriarch of the Polish Holy Order—talk to a corpse. *One foot at a time, okay, Filip?* Elza's mother's fingers twitch at her side, like she's about to draw her sword or take out a cigarette.

"Has Father called yet?" Elza asks her.

"He'll call when his work is done," Marzena replies. "And not a moment before."

Elza wonders if that's why Dymitr hasn't called her back—because his mission isn't finished yet. But she doesn't think he has that much in common with their parents, so single-minded they think only of whatever they need to kill next, instead of considering their family. Her cheeks suddenly hot, she steps outside, and leans against the railing.

It's after sunset. The outdoor lights are on, and flies are buzzing around them. The air is cooler now, the breeze ruffling her hair. Soon all the cousins and aunts and uncles will pile into their cars and come here, parking on the lawn and crowding into the house. Elza will pass out the sheet music and everyone will start singing. And eating. And singing. And drinking. They'll fill the house with noise and activity so no one has to be alone with Filip's body.

Elza hasn't fought a strzyga yet. They would never admit it—especially not her grandmother—but they don't send women who can still bear children out on the risky missions, most of the time. A woman Knight has two responsibilities: hunt monsters and make more Knights. Even Marzena, who doesn't have a maternal bone in her body, knew that. She had three children when she probably would have preferred none.

So Elza's taken down a zmora, a wraith, and two rusałkas. But she's helped countless others track their own quarry. She's a better tracker than Dymitr or Kazik, though she couldn't beat either of them in a fight, much to her mother's constant disappointment. "You have to work twice as hard as them because you're weaker," Marzena said to her once. "But don't think for a moment that you don't have the capacity to beat them."

It was one of the nicer things Marzena ever said to her.

Elza sees a shadow along the tree line. Her hand is just going to the back of her neck, ready to draw one of her swords, when the outdoor light stretches across his face.

"Dymitr!" she says, in a gasp. She runs down the steps and across the gravel to fling her arms around her brother.

If she'd thought for a moment longer, she might have been more uncertain. He was so strange to her the last time they spoke, so cruel. *You are an encumbrance. You are a burden.* And then ordering her to go home like she was an annoying kid tagging along with her older brother instead of a Knight, instead of his partner. *Go home, Elza, or the next time I see you I will kill you myself.*

But he wraps his arms around her now. He feels different to her, not as sturdy. She holds him at arm's length, frowning.

"Did you lose weight?" she asks him. "Is it stress?"

He's on an important mission, after all. And he looks so tired.

"Maybe," he says, with a weak smile. "How are you?"

"Oh, you know." She wants to make a joke of it, but she can't think of anything. She just lets the phrase hang over them both.

"I do."

Her eyes burn. She looks back at the house.

"The singing will start soon," she says. "Do you think he could really turn into something?"

The old stories said a body left undefended after death could turn into a wraith, or an upiór, or a wieszczy. The Holy Order knows, now, that wraiths are born, not made. But upiórs seem to spring from nothing and nowhere, and wieszczy are too rare, too mysterious, to be certain of them.

"It seems silly to me, to be so afraid of an impossible transformation that you'd sing all night," she says.

"Maybe it's not so impossible," Dymitr says. "Or maybe the singing isn't for him."

She held back the tears in the car with their mother, and she tries to hold them back again now, but it's hard around Dymitr. They've always been each other's refuge in vulnerable moments. When Dymitr came back from his first kill, inconsolable, she was the one who calmed him down. When she lost her first sparring match against their cousin Agnieszka and their grandmother called Elza's performance "pathetic," Dymitr dragged her out to the woods to sit in their childhood fort so she could cry in peace. They let each other see the things they don't reveal to anyone else. But she doesn't want to do that now.

She blinks the tears away.

"I take it you didn't finish your mission," she says coolly.

"No, I had to . . . change my plan."

"Because of me?"

He doesn't answer for a little too long. Well, of course it was because of her. She revealed to those *things* he was with—the strzygoń and the zmora—that he was a Knight. He was probably using them to get into Baba Jaga's apartment, and she ruined it for him.

"Come on, let's go inside," she says. "Mother's in a foul mood, but I'm sure she'll be nicer to you than she was to me."

"Maybe. Maybe not. We both know it's Kazik she really loves."

It's an old joke. Kazik is as cold and unsentimental as Marzena is.

"I'm sorry, Elza," he says, taking her by the elbow so she doesn't walk away from him.

He's always looked like her twin. Ash-brown hair.

Gray eyes. Big lips—like a fish, Kazik used to tease them, sucking his cheeks in to imitate one. The resemblance weakened as Dymitr got older and started filling out and growing facial hair, but still, there's no mistaking that he's her brother. Only now . . . there's something different about his eyes. A kind of wildness she doesn't understand. It makes her feel uneasy.

"For what?" she says, even though she knows what he's apologizing for. She'd rather not hear the specifics, though it does relieve some of the tension in her, to hear that he's sorry.

"For all of it," he answers.

"It's good you're here" is all she says, and they walk together toward the house.

A FEAST FOR THE DEAD

He steps into the living room, and the scents of the house overwhelm him. Cooked cabbage in the kitchen. Rose perfume clinging to his aunt Krystyna's clothes. Nalewka and cigarettes on someone's breath. Dirt. Blood.

Death.

And those are just the smells that any person with a decent nose could detect. There's also the peach-sweet aroma of anticipation, the dark-chocolate richness of dread, the powdered sugar of anxiety. All the fear-scents of his cousins, his siblings, his mother—

But he can't think about the smell, or about Nikodem Kostka, zemsta, prowling the woods outside the house in pursuit of Knight blood. He can't think about whether he's more afraid that Niko will fail, or that he'll succeed. He has to focus.

He murmurs condolences in his aunt's ear. Krystyna's cloying perfume is in his nose, and beneath it, a peculiar vanilla smell that he thinks might be grief. *No one ever told me that grief felt so like fear,* isn't that a quote from C. S. Lewis? Only a zmora could confirm it, it seems.

Krystyna's hand, when she pats his cheek, is cold and a little damp, and he realizes she was just washing the body. It's as if she left a handprint of death on his face. He can smell it even when she pulls away.

"So here you are," a familiar voice says from behind him, flinty. Marzena. His mother.

She smells like copper and leather. Not a small woman, but not a tall one, either. Her dark brown hair is limp and loose over her shoulders, and her gray eyes are exactly like his.

Will they be the last thing Niko sees before she dies? Before *he* dies?

"I thought you were on an important mission," Marzena says. "You failed?"

"No," Dymitr replies. "I'm still in the middle of it."

He considered his story carefully as he walked through the woods on his way to the house, Ala at his side. He couldn't tell them he'd failed, because failing a mission to kill Baba Jaga would mean his death. He also couldn't tell them he'd succeeded. And though it pained him to admit it, the best excuse he could give for leaving in the middle of his mission was to imply that Elza derailed him. That it was a good time to leave and regroup, because he would have to start all over again, thanks to his sister's ill-timed interventions.

Regardless, it's not typical for a Knight to take a break in the middle of a mission, as if theirs is a job that offers paid leave and vacation days. But then, a mission like his—to find and kill the most powerful witch who's ever lived—is not typical, either.

"So, important enough to take you across the world, but not important enough to keep you there after a set-back," Marzena supplies, and all around them people are pretending not to hear, the young cousins chopping herbs at the kitchen table, Krystyna squeezing out the wet rag she used to clean Filip's body, Elza studying the wall clock.

Ten years ago, or maybe even five years ago, he would have cowered in response to Marzena's disapproval. But once his grandmother started teaching him, paying attention to him, encouraging him, he found that his mother no longer had that power.

So he says, "Patience is not a fault."

"It is when it's a disguise for dawdling. I thought we taught you better."

"Perhaps I simply don't remember what *you* taught me, given how sparse your lessons were."

Marzena sneers. She opens her mouth to reply, and the creaky voice of Dymitr's grandmother speaks from the living room.

"Enough of that," she says, and he turns to face her.

His memories of Joanna diminished her. She's no ordinary old woman in floral-patterned blouses, with rings on her age-spotted hands. She stands upright and sturdy in old work boots, her silver hair in a tight braid. She may be too old to draw her bone sword, but she's far from finished.

He hears Baba Jaga's voice in his ears. *Thirty-three swords drawn from the spines of the dead . . . you will begin with the one you call Babcia.*

"Dymek," his grandmother says to him.

"Babcia," he replies.

She gestures for him to come to her, and he does, bending his head so she can press a kiss to his cheek. She smells like the ginger-and-clove muscle balm she uses on her arthritic hands, and the bergamot in her perfume, and the death that clings to her fingers. She doesn't smell like fear, not even a trace of it.

"You're different," she says quietly.

Fear pulses in his chest and makes his skin prickle. There's no way she can know, he reminds himself. She can't identify a zmora with human sight alone. She *can't.*

"I wish I had better news of my mission to lessen the sorrow of the occasion," he says, because he thinks it's what he would have said, before. Back when his successes felt urgent, like they might save humanity.

It's the right thing to say. Her eyes soften, and she pats his arm.

"Great works take time. Get your grandfather's rosary from my dresser. We'll wrap it around Filip's hands."

He nods, and walks through the living room to the bedroom beyond it. Despite telling Ala that he knew this would be fine, he's trembling with relief.

He always liked funerals, as a child. He didn't really understand what they meant back then. Everyone talked about the deceased person being with God, and dying in service to humanity, both of which sounded like good things, so though funerals always had a few people crying at them, he was never sure why. The permanence of death hadn't yet become clear to him.

What he liked was that they felt like holidays: a full house, a warm kitchen, everyone busy, music in the air. He wore a black suit even when he was a child, and though it was itchy and heavy on his shoulders, he liked that it made him look like one of the adults, and he liked that his grandfather or his father would polish his shoes, liked the smell of the polish and the way they spit on the leather and the little brush they used to do it while the shoes were still on his feet. He liked to sit at one of the little tables they'd pushed together to make one long one, and eat łazanki until he was much too full.

Even now, some of what he loved as a child lingers on, as he goes with Elza to the trunk in her bedroom where all the fine linens are kept and takes out a big stack of them so they can spread them over all the tables—the little round one from the living room where their grandmother takes her afternoon tea, and the kitchen table, and the folding table the cousins take out when they play cards, and the desk from Dymitr's bedroom. They don't say much, but she points out the little stains, *from when Piotr made Kazik laugh and chocolate milk came out of his nose at Easter dinner, remember?* And *that year Filip and Krystyna fought about whether the tree was crooked or not, and Krystyna gestured so hard she knocked over a glass of wine.*

He's used to the ache of his missing sword, but a new one joins it now. When he was in Chicago, it was easy to pretend that he didn't miss his family, that he didn't *love them*; it was easy to focus on what they were instead of who they were to him. But now he watches the youngest cousin, André, in the kitchen, spots on his cheeks, stirring up sour cream; now he watches Kazik wiping down chairs from the storage shed to get the cobwebs off; now he sees Joanna nudging Marzena with her shoulder as they line up the tables, and he remembers.

He remembers that Knights, like the creatures they hunt, are people.

His people.

So he aches, even as he casts a long look at the bathroom sink where the book of curses is hidden. If Elza wasn't with him, he could grab it, and there would be no need for Ala to come into this house at all. But his sister is waiting for him at the end of the hallway, her arms piled high with linens, so he follows her to the living room. He has to stick to the plan he made with Ala.

He just hopes Niko doesn't derail it.

Everyone shows up after dark, squeezed into old cars that he recognizes from a decade ago, in some cases. They're dressed in black, and the older women wear scarves over their hair, and the older men shuffle in on unsteady feet. Cousins, second cousins, great-uncles and -aunts. The family is big, though not all of them can make it; he doesn't recognize half of them, though some of them know him by reputation. Like the old man who squints at him from the doorway, holding his hat against his stomach, and then nods in greeting.

"Curse-bearer," the man says.

When Joanna gave him the book of curses, she told him it was a secret—and it is, because no one else in the family is supposed to lay eyes on it. But the fact that he has it in his possession is not a secret anymore. She told everyone last Christmas, so they knew how the knowledge was being passed down. Dymitr still remembers how Kazik looked at him, then, like he'd betrayed his older brother in some profound way, by being the one she chose. It was the same way Dymitr had looked at Kazik, once, when their father decided to train him.

"Sir," he says, with a nod.

He doesn't want to talk about the curses. It only makes him think of Ala, who will be taking a huge risk, helping him tonight. Retrieving the book isn't as simple as grabbing it and tucking it under his waistband—it's too big for that, and too powerful to go undetected. It would only draw attention.

He slips into the kitchen, where his older cousin, Agnieszka, is chopping a cooked sausage to go in the łazanki. Her shirt is too big for her, and it's slipped down her shoulder to reveal the sliver of gold from the hilt of the bone sword. She looks back at him.

"How was America?" she asks him. "Did you see the Empire State Building?"

"That's in a different part of the country," he says, smiling a little. "Chicago has some nice buildings, though."

"I've always wanted to go there." She winks. "Maybe you need a partner for your mission?"

He looks across the room at Elza, who's arranging the chrysanthemums someone brought in a vase.

"It's something that has to be done alone, I'm afraid," he says. "How are the kids?"

Agnieszka beams as she talks about her twin sons, who both love soccer, even though one of them kicks hard, but can barely run without tripping over his feet, and the other is fast, but always misses the ball.

She says, "Together, they would make one good player. Separately, they're terrible."

He laughs, and Elza thrusts another bouquet of chrysanthemums at him. They're a deep fuchsia, their petals narrow and pointed. He thinks of the fern flower, and how it unfurled so elegantly, like a ballerina's skirt as she turns. He remembers how it tasted, green, almost herbal. And how it burned the darkness from his blood, and then transferred that cleansing fire to Ala.

"God, I hate these," Elza says, of the chrysanthemums. "Especially the purple ones. How did they end up becoming the official funeral flower, anyway? They're worse than carnations."

"I like carnations."

Elza nods. "Oh, I remember. You gave Celina Nowak a bouquet of them on Valentine's Day once, remember?"

He makes a face. That was before he realized that thinking a girl was pretty and wanting to sleep with her were two different things—and he only felt the former. "That's right—the petals were dyed blue. She was very polite about them."

"And then she very politely stuck her tongue in Bartek Adamczyk's mouth later that day," Kazik says, clapping Dymitr on the shoulder. He's holding two small glasses of clear liquor. "Let's drink."

"None for me?" Elza says, pouting her lower lip a little.

"Oh, they're both for you," Kazik says, putting both glasses in her hands. "You think I don't remember how you can drink? You put us both to shame that one Christmas. What were we drinking? Vodka?"

"Jägermeister," Elza says, with an exaggerated shudder. "I still can't have licorice. That's all I tasted when it was on its way back up."

Kazik goes to pour another glass, and Elza gives Dymitr one of her two. They stand in a triangle in the kitchen, on the laminate floor, and touch their glasses together.

"Prost," Kazik says.

"Santé," Elza says.

"Cheers," Dymitr says, with a weak smile.

And then, in unison: "Na zdrowie!"

They all drink, and Dymitr thinks it was a mistake, coming back here. A month ago, when he set out for Chicago, he thought he was going to his death—or near enough to it. If Baba Jaga had done as he asked, and destroyed his bone sword—and half of his soul—he would have wandered the earth diminished, in a haze of pain and emptiness. The Knights who had suffered that fate in the past hadn't been able to articulate it except in verbal accounts, since they lost the ability to write afterward. What little they were able to describe was a miserable kind of detachment from their own bodies. They were capable of basic functioning, but no connection—no emotion, and no relief.

He wouldn't have cared, then, about his siblings or his cousins or his grandmother. He wouldn't have cared about anything at all.

But now, he'll have to say goodbye to them knowing they would hate him if they knew what he really was. Knowing that he'll only ever be able to lie to them. Knowing that he still loves them, no matter what they've done, and no matter what lies they've believed.

And how can he blame them? He believed those lies, too.

It's strange to eat with a body in the next room, but they do, squeezed in so tightly Dymitr can hardly move his fork without elbowing Agnieszka. In the living room, a few people are already singing hymns to keep the evil spirits at bay. Elza gives him pained looks across the table whenever the singing voices hit the wrong note—which is often— and he tries not to laugh. Their mother, on Elza's right, appraises him.

"Your sister says you were awfully comfortable around the local population when she saw you," Marzena says.

In this context, *local population* doesn't refer to humans, but to creatures. *Quasi-mortals*. Ala also calls them "monsters" with a kind of fondness, like she's referring to a pesky little brother—but he doesn't think the word would sound the same, coming from his mouth.

"We all have our sources," Dymitr says.

"True," Marzena acknowledges. "Some more tolerable than others."

Dymitr slides his phone out of his pocket, and with a surreptitious glance at the cousin beside him, unlocks it.

"What was the one in town you told me about, Mother?" Kazik asks her. "The one who could barely keep its spit in its mouth."

"It was a wieszczy, and I'll thank you not to remind me of its spitting habit. I had to shower after talking to it," Marzena says. "But it gave me a czart that turned out to be a windfall. I'm going to go back in a few months, see if it will give me anything else. And if not . . ." She turns her knife over her fingers, a small smile on her face. "All sources become targets, eventually. I hope you didn't get attached, boy."

Dymitr thinks of the czart he saw in the strzyga club,

with his small horns and even smaller smile, like he was keeping a fond secret. He keeps his voice steady as he says, "My heart isn't as soft as you imagine."

"Tell that to the mice you used to cry over," Kazik says, with a grin.

Dymitr looks down, like he's embarrassed, only it's just an excuse to look at his phone. He pulls up his messages, and opens the text chain he started with Ala earlier that day. With a few taps, he's sent Ala the message they agreed on: a book emoji.

While he's here at dinner, and certain that everyone is too busy to notice a hole in the house's magic, Ala will sneak in through his old bedroom window and retrieve the book of curses from its hiding place. She'll be gone before anyone feels its absence. Not that they would know where to search for a magical disruption like that anyway—only he knows where he put it, and only Elza knows to look under the bathroom sink.

"In his defense, I had just watched *Cinderella,*" Elza says. "Maybe the cartoon mice made too much of an impact on him."

Dymitr rolls his eyes and puts his phone back in his pocket.

"It wasn't because of *Cinderella,*" Joanna says, from farther down the table. She speaks a little coolly, as she often does when she hears Kazik taunting him. "It was because the traps didn't usually kill the mice, and he didn't like to watch them suffer."

Dymitr has a vivid memory of one of the mice with its hips trapped under the metal bar, broken. It was scrambling with its front legs, its eyes bulging. He can hardly keep himself from wincing at the thought of it, even now.

Joanna goes on: "I explained to him that killing them was a mercy—that death is not the worst that awaits any creature, but suffering. He handled them well enough after that."

"It shouldn't be so hard, to kill something with no soul," Marzena points out. "Not for us."

Joanna says, "The things we hunt, they are clever in their deceptions. They convince us of their morality, their vulnerability, their wholeness. He pitied the mouse because he imagined it had a human's awareness of doom, a human's understanding of suffering. It's because the monstrous things of this world remind us of *humanity* that some of our number pity them. And we need Knights who have an acute awareness of humanity, or we will become as twisted as the evil things are."

These kinds of speeches used to make Dymitr's heart swell in his chest like a balloon. They used to make him feel not only that he belonged in the Holy Order, but that he was an integral part of it, offering it something that no one else could. Before, his grandmother's speeches could make him shake off frustration and press through pain, they made him go eagerly to the weapons room to do penance, they made him pore over every detail of every mission to ensure he hadn't missed anything, until the early hours of the morning.

Now, he feels cold, all the way to the core of him, as Joanna focuses on Dymitr, a solemn look on her lined face.

"If he falters in his belief," she says, "it's his task to do penance to correct the flaw in his heart."

And he had, hadn't he? He knelt on dry peas for hours. He prayed as he mortified his flesh with holy magic. He begged whatever and whoever was listening to wrench the doubt out of his heart by force and firm his resolve.

Joanna looks at her daughter, then, adding: "But if you have no human heart, Marzena, you must do penance as well."

Marzena looks down at her plate. For once, she looks almost ashamed. Kazik offers Dymitr a nod of apology. The silence is strained, and then there's the sound of footsteps outside, and the door shivers as someone pounds on it with a heavy fist. For a terrible, irrational moment, he thinks it's Niko coming to kill his mother or die trying. Then it opens, and standing on the mat is Dymitr's father, Łukasz.

He's a tall man, as tall as Dymitr and Kazik, but broader and sturdier, with a thick beard and ash-brown hair that's thinning at the temples. He has round, shallow-set eyes that seem to bulge when he widens them. But now his face is pinched with fatigue and grief.

Joanna rises to greet him, and slowly, the others rise to

do the same. Filip and Łukasz went on missions together often; they were as close as twins, each one half of a whole. Though Krystyna is Filip's wife, it's Łukasz who carries the most grief for his brother, felled by a strzyga.

As Dymitr watches his cousins giving his father a warm welcome, he thinks of Nikodem Kostka, his eyes like lit embers, his curve of a smile.

Some people move into the living room to join the singers, clearing a space in the middle of the table for Łukasz to sit. He piles a plate high with food: łazanki with breaded pork nestled beside it, red cabbage and mashed potatoes with sour cream and dill. He skips the pierogi, which André is already eyeing hungrily.

"Well, now that Łukasz is here, you must tell us the tale," Joanna says to Marzena.

Marzena doesn't seem like a natural storyteller. She's curt and impatient with foolishness. But war stories are different—they bring out another side of her, one that's lively and engaging. Dymitr has always liked his mother best when she was telling stories.

In the next room, the singers drone on, and the mournful tune is, somehow, the perfect background music for the tale of Filip's strzyga.

A RESTLESS SPIRIT

Ala crouches next to a pine tree, her phone in her hand so she doesn't miss the signal. One hundred yards in front of her is the house of Knights, lit up like a lantern against the night. She can see shadows shifting behind the lace curtains of each window. The gravel driveway is packed with cars.

She watched them all arrive from her place in the trees, kneeling in the dirt to make sure she wasn't visible over the brush. Despite knowing they couldn't see her, she still quaked with terror at the sight of so many of them. They were too far away for her to recognize them, but she suspects she would, if she saw them up close—she would know their faces from the memories that once played for her every morning like a horror film.

She's glad she didn't see them up close.

All around her is the cool, humid air and the buzz of insects and the rustling of birds in the trees. She hears music coming from the house, a dirge that reminds her of going to church with her mother as a child, with an itchy dress on and shoes that pinched her toes. Her mother insisted on going every Sunday until Ala was fourteen, and when Ala asked her why, she said that some days it was an act of devotion, and some days it was an act of defiance. *The Holy Order doesn't get to decide who receives salvation and who doesn't,* her mother said. *They don't get to take this from us.* Ala agreed with the sentiment, even if she didn't share her mother's faith.

Behind her, she hears voices from somewhere among the trees. Her stomach gives a lurch. She draws the knife at her hip and turns her back on the house of Knights, creeping into the darkness to see what's going on.

She doesn't have to go far. There's a small pond a dozen yards behind her, and there are two figures at the edge of it, one crouched and one . . . strange.

A cloud passes over the moon, and in the clarity of the moonlight Ala sees them for what they are. A girl— but not just a girl. She has lanky arms and acne-spotted cheeks, and there's a body growing out of her spine, like a plant sprouting from a crack in a stone. Black fabric swirls around the body, and instead of a human head, a human face, all Ala can see is a skull.

They're back-to-back, the girl and *whatever it is,* attached at the spine and facing two different directions. It's the girl, though, who's holding a sword to a man's throat.

The man isn't facing her head-on, so it takes her a moment to recognize that he's Niko.

She knew Niko was going on a hunt, but she never imagined he'd turn up here, in the same town where

Dymitr's grandmother lives—or that he would turn up *here,* in the woods right behind the woman's house, when the entire family is gathered inside it. The sight of him is so incongruous, in fact, that all she can do is gape at him as he kneels in the dirt at the mercy of this two-bodied thing. *Badass zemsta my ass.*

"If you are planning to go inside the cockroach nest, you should say so," the girl is saying to Niko. As her mouth moves, the mouth of the skull behind her also moves, the teeth clattering together in a gruesome imitation of speech. "Because I have no use for a means of conveyance that's about to die."

The girl's voice is high and young. As a cloud passes over the moon, the body attached to the girl's back disappears, as if it was never there.

Ala's phone buzzes in her pocket; Dymitr is giving her the signal. But she can't leave now, not until she knows Niko is safe. And she doesn't want to step out of the relative safety of the trees until she knows what this thing is.

She also wants to spit curses at Niko, because he's currently, at this very moment, fucking everything up for her.

"You wouldn't like possessing me," Niko says. "My life is too full of danger. You should find someone more boring. A shopkeeper, maybe, or a farmer—"

Ala's heard of possessing spirits. Too many, in fact; people all over the world believe in spirits. She's most familiar with the idea of demon possession, something her mother didn't believe in, but other Catholic zmoras seem to. *We exist, so why not demons?* Even if they're wrong about the particulars, they seem to agree that the possessing spirit is malicious, like a host-devouring parasite.

There are other spirits, though, that seem to be neutral, or even beneficial to the host. She has no idea what this one is, though given the knife she's holding to Niko's throat, she's betting on "malicious."

"You don't know what I'd *like*," the girl says, her voice now impossibly deep. "So few of my people are left in this place, and even fewer of my kind. No one knows me, not even when they try to draw magic from the land and it twists in their hands. No one is left to know what I want."

The girl turns her head and spits. Then she leans down to whisper into Niko's ear, and her voice is so deep that it carries over to where Ala stands among the trees.

"You think I want a quiet life? I don't want a life at all." She turns the blade so it catches the light of the moon. Niko's next swallow is labored. "I already lived. Now I want what comes after. And you're going to get me there."

Ala still doesn't know what this is, but she's running out of time. She steps forward, into the moonlight.

"Sorry to interrupt," she says. "But I feel like I should point out that if you were going to possess him, you would have done it already. Which means either your threat is empty, or . . . that you can't do it."

The girl looks up at her. As it so often is, it's the eyes that give her away. She doesn't look at Ala the way a normal teenage girl would—wary, maybe, or bored, or curious. She looks at Ala like she's tired. Worn down by the world.

"I can," the girl says.

Niko lets out a short laugh.

"You can't," Ala says, as calmly as she can manage. "The only reason you're still alive is because your host is a child, and my friend doesn't want to kill her. Congratulations, by the way, that's a new level of fucked up."

"Ala, the host is still alive under there," Niko says in English, and it takes effort for her to understand him, like her ears have almost forgotten the words. "I can hear her heart."

The phone in Ala's pocket is like a stone weighing her down. She has to *go*. She can't go.

The girl glares at her. "I didn't want this host. I had no choice—I was exhausted."

"'I didn't have a choice.' Everyone's favorite excuse for ruining someone else's life," Ala says. "So what do you want, exactly? A new host?"

Niko looks exasperated. One of his hands is raised, as if in surrender, and she can see something strapped to his arm—a weapon, probably. He hasn't moved to draw it.

Of course he hasn't. If the host is still alive, there must be a way to save her. They just have to convince the possessing spirit to let her go.

The girl bites her lip in a surprisingly human gesture.

"I'm tired," she says quietly. "So tired of wandering. So tired of running."

"What is it, exactly?" Niko asks Ala, again in English.

Ala almost remembers. Her mother had a boyfriend, once—a German creature cousin to the zmora, an alp. He'd spent his youth traveling, and he liked to talk about all the strange things he'd come across. In Northern Canada, an ijiraq, a shapeshifter rumored to steal children—a myth, of course, and the source of too much trouble. A Tata Duende, a forest guardian in Belize with no thumbs and an affinity for braiding. And . . .

"Dybbuk," she says, the word surfacing from her mind like a crossword clue. A dybbuk, a Jewish spirit—*So few of my people are left in this place, and even fewer of my kind.*

The girl visibly tenses.

"A wandering spirit," Ala goes on. "Whose sin in life was so great they lingered after death, seeking restitution." She pauses, considering this. "And you thought having a zemsta as a host would give you access to that restitution."

"I'm tired of wandering," the girl—the dybbuk, really—says. The clouds pull away from the moon again, so Ala can see the body attached to the girl's back, the swirling black cloak and the chattering skull. "I want what comes after."

"Then leave him here," Ala says. "Leave the girl, too. Come with me into the house of Knights." Niko opens his mouth to object, and she holds up a hand to silence him, focused on the girl. "Attach yourself to one of them, instead."

The girl recoils, and Niko takes the opportunity to

slip from her grasp, stumbling away from her to the edge of the pond. In an instant his blade is drawn, but there's no need—the girl is clutching her knife to her chest, her shoulders hunched in.

"I can't," the girl says. "Their split souls—"

"Then find one who hasn't made a sword yet. Walk their feet on a different path." Ala steps closer. "*Save a soul.* Won't that be enough?"

"You don't know what I did." The unnaturally deep voice sounds desperate now. "I need—*vengeance.* Not—"

"If you stop a Knight from becoming a Knight, you don't just save their soul," Ala says. "You save everyone they would have killed. You can't tell me vengeance would be better than that."

The girl looks down. She's wearing such ordinary clothes. Blue jeans that are too loose on her, white sneakers streaked with mud from the walk through the woods. A zip-up sweatshirt with fraying hood strings.

"You'll carry me into the house?" she asks.

"Ala," Niko says sharply. "You can't—"

"I'll carry you in . . . but only if you give me your name," Ala says. There's power in a name, and she can use it to expel the spirit if it doesn't keep its word.

The girl sinks to her knees in the mud. Though there's still a cloud over the moon now, the creature with its black cloak and tangled hair appears.

"Adam," the dybbuk says.

The girl shudders, and then wrenches upright, her back

bowing, arching. With a crack that makes Ala wince, the dybbuk breaks from the girl, and Niko lunges to catch her as she falls forward.

But Ala's focus is on the shadow thing, on the dybbuk, as it clambers over to her. It walks like it bears a great weight, favoring one leg. The empty pits where its eyes were are focused on her; she can feel them, even if there's nothing to see. Its teeth click, and Ala offers it a hand. She can't stop herself from shaking.

The dybbuk doesn't grab her. Instead, with a swirl of its cloak, it spins and disappears. She feels a weight settle on her shoulders—heavy, but not more than she can bear. She hears its whisper in her ear, and the click of its teeth.

"Keep your promise, zmora," it says.

"You've lost your mind," Niko says, scowling at her. The host—the girl, now—is at his feet, lying on her side. He checks her wrist for a pulse, and then steps over her. "I know you came here to help Dymitr, but you can't go into that house, with or without a fucking . . . *ghost* on your back."

Ala takes her phone from her pocket. The message from Dymitr is waiting for her—the book emoji.

Maybe it's not too late.

"I can't?" Ala says. "That's funny, because I'm about to."

She takes off into the trees. Niko follows her.

"They're *all* in there," Niko says. "And you don't know what they're capable of—"

The rage is so sudden she chokes on it. She turns back to

him, scowling, and says, "I don't know what they're capable of? I, who bore their curse, who watched their crimes day after day after day, *I* don't know what they're capable of?"

Niko holds up his hands, palms facing her.

"You're right, you're right," he says. "That was a stupid thing to say. I'm sorry. I just—I'm about to create chaos. And I can't guarantee that what you're planning will still work, in the midst of that. So I think you should find another way to help him."

"I didn't come here to help him. I have my own reasons for being here, and if the outcome happens to help him, good. But I'm here for me." She feels the press of the knife against her back, where it's sheathed. "I want that book, so none of them can ever curse a family like mine again. And I want—"

She can't say that she's here to kill Joanna Myśliwiec out loud. It would sound too absurd to Nikodem Kostka, strzygoń zemsta, trained fighter. He knows she's more capable than most zmora to defend herself, but no one thinks a zmora can fight a Knight, not really. Not even most zmoras. They're better at running, at hiding. Fast, evasive, clever—that's what a zmora is supposed to be. To march into a house full of Knights and try to kill their matriarch is madness.

But Ala isn't going to try to be a powerful warrior. She's going to do this as a zmora: fast, evasive.

Clever.

"I want my nightmares to stop," Ala says quietly. "And in order to do that, I can't keep running from the cause of them. I have to face her."

From the stricken look on Niko's face, she thinks maybe he never considered that. Maybe he thought the curse ended when Dymitr broke it with the fern flower. Maybe he thought the memories of what the curse showed her would spill out of her like water from an ear after swimming, in a rush of heat as she slept.

"You'll probably die," Niko says to her, gently.

"You'll probably die, too," she says. "But I don't see *you* refusing to do what you have to. Why do you expect me to?"

Niko lowers his hands. There's a troubled set to his mouth. But he nods.

"You've got five minutes before all hell breaks loose," he says. "So . . . hurry."

With the dybbuk's weight on her back, she turns back to the house of Knights, to the pit of vipers, and she hopes the busy brightness of the house means she isn't too late to follow Dymitr's signal.

A TALE OF TWINS

"Filip had been tracking the strzyga for some time," Elza's mother begins, running a hand over the tablecloth. The guests rearrange themselves around the table, some of them taking the places of the singers in the next room, and Kazik grabbing his car keys so a sober cousin can drive him to his shift at the cemetery. He'll be guarding Filip's plot until morning.

Marzena leans forward to draw the attention of all the young people at the table, and most of the older ones, too. Elza remembers this side of her mother, holding court at the dinner table when she got home from a mission, still wearing her gear even though it made Łukasz roll his eyes. No one could deny her when she was like this, her eyes alight with victory.

As a child Elza tried to invite stories even when that light wasn't in Marzena's eyes—*Tell us again about the połódnica in Warsaw!*—and Marzena would snap at her. *Can't I get any goddamn peace, girl,* she would say, and Elza has always hated being called "girl" as a result.

Marzena continues: "There were rumors of a small

strzyga clan in Szczecin, and he believed killing their leader would force them to scatter across the region, so that he could pick them off one by one."

Elza nods along with her words. It's the same strategy Filip taught her: only a fool goes after a group of strzygas without destabilizing them first, and a Knight shouldn't also be a fool. Wisdom lies in identifying the clan's leader and luring her away from the others. The clan will then disintegrate into infighting, since none of the remaining strzygas will be willing to cede power to the others, and it's easier to hunt them individually.

"He found one of them, but Filip was a patient man. He followed it for days through the city without it knowing, and on the fifth day, he permitted it to catch sight of him, so that it would call a meeting of its associates. And it did—at the home of the strzyga leader. An older one, with the pale yellow eyes of an owl, and eyebrows that crawled into each other."

Marzena leans toward one of the young cousins and puts her finger up to bridge the gap between her eyebrows, to show her what Marzena means. The little girl giggles.

"Do strzygas sound like owls, Aunt?" the girl asks her.

"Sure they do!" Marzena replies, and she makes a hooting sound.

Łukasz sets a hand on the girl's arm and shakes his head, to tell her Marzena is only joking, but he has a crooked smile on his face. Even glum Łukasz isn't immune to Marzena's charms; it's why they got married in the first place, though Elza has a hard time imagining their court-ship to be anything but perfunctory.

Marzena goes on. "Filip waited for the meeting to fin-ish, and then he followed the strzyga leader, who he called 'Athene' after the owl breed *Athene noctua*. Only Athene must have been cleverer than he knew, because it spotted him."

"How?" Elza asks sharply. Filip wasn't careless, the way some of their number are. He kept meticulous notes and took twice as long on missions as anyone else. He also rarely had the close calls that others in the Holy Order had. In the last ten years, he'd gotten injured only once.

"His notebook didn't say." Marzena shrugs. "But Athene ran, and Filip followed it. He chased it across the border to Berlin, where it joined up with another clan, who ferried it down through Leipzig and Frankfurt. As long as it was with them, he wrote, it was untouchable. So he decided to lay a trap, instead."

Even if Dymitr hadn't told Ala which room was his, she would have known it by the smell. It's not that it smells like him, though it does—it smells like him, mixed with copper and earth, the scents that all Knights seem to have in common. No—it's because it smells like orange peel.

The scent has taken over Ala's apartment in the weeks since Dymitr started living there. He has few indulgences, but oranges are among them, and he leaves the peels on the coffee table, on the kitchen counter, and even, on one occasion, on the bookshelf. His fingernails are always yellow from them. So though it's been a month or more since he was last in his bedroom, she can still smell the orange peels in the trash can.

She shifts uncomfortably—the dybbuk is heavy; she has no idea how that teenage girl bore it for so long. She doesn't have time to look around, but she can't help it. She looks at his nightstand, where a Bible waits as well as an empty glass, for water, and a small bowl with dry peas in it. She puzzles over the latter for a few seconds before moving to the bookcase, where there's a shelf of small plastic figurines: a dinosaur, a dragon, a spider, a tiger. As far as she can tell, they're the room's only adornment. It's otherwise sparse, like a guest room.

She feels a pang, thinking of a younger Dymitr keeping everything he thinks, everything he feels, inside his own head because it's not safe to say out loud. Even in the memory she shared with him, she saw how honesty was punished with penance. *Ten times,* his grandmother instructed him, and Ala is sure that means he had to hurt himself—in exactly what way, she doesn't know. But it makes sense, now, why it's so easy for Dymitr to ignore the ache of his missing sword. His life has been replete with pain.

Ala opens the door an inch to peer into the hallway. She needs to make sure the coast is clear before she leaves the room.

"Filip picked off one of the younger members of the German clan and left an invitation in its place," says a cold, clear voice, faint enough that Ala can barely make sense of it. "*Come alone,* he wrote, *and you can have your youngling back alive.*"

Ala recoils. She's seen so many horrors inflicted by Knights. Children murdered in their beds, or made to watch as their parents died. She thought she was desensitized to it. But the way this Knight speaks, it's not as if she's talking about animals. A Knight hunting creatures believing they're like animals would, in some ways, be understandable—humans hunt animals all the time.

But no—this Knight sounds like she knows *exactly* what she's hunting.

And she doesn't care.

🐿

In the next room, just a few voices sing the hymns to keep the evil spirits at bay, their voices low and creaking.

"Filip picked off one of the younger members of the German clan and left an invitation in its place. *Come alone,* he wrote, *and you can have your youngling back alive.* He knew, of course, that Athene would never come to him alone. But he went to the Black Forest, where the trees are so dense that sunlight hardly penetrates to the ground below, and he laid false trails for Athene to follow. Then he waited by the edge of the forest to watch the clan arrive, Athene among them."

Elza glances at Dymitr, who looks just as rapt as the others, his eyes fixed on his mother's face. Only his face is drained of color, despite the warmth in the little house. He looks almost . . . afraid. And no wonder: his mission is to kill Baba Jaga, a far more dangerous target than Filip's. Filip's death must be a sobering reminder of just how vulnerable they all are.

"Filip followed Athene through the woods and drew his sword once he was under the cover of trees." Marzena holds her hands behind her head, as if she's about to draw her own bone sword; Elza remembers it well, a saber, a little curved, the blade bright white. "I followed his trail of blood deep into the woods, and there I found his body. Only there was something peculiar around the body—the feathers of an owl, of course, but *two* sets of footprints instead of one."

The young cousins are staring now, wild-eyed.

"For a long time I puzzled over this," Marzena says. "One set of footprints leading through the woods, with Filip's behind. One set of footprints leading away from his body. But two distinct sets surrounding him in the clearing where he was killed. How did two strzygas appear where there was only one, before? And how could I determine which set of tracks to follow out of the clearing?"

"You looked at the tread of the shoes?" Elza prompts her.

"Someone is eager to race ahead," Marzena says, disapproving, but she's smiling. "Yes, I looked at the tread of its shoes, and found them to be identical—another oddity. But then I realized they weren't actually identical. In one set of footprints, the tread was worn all the way down in the heel, but only on the left foot. In the other set, the tread was worn just the same way, but in the right foot. One strzyga was the mirror image of the other."

"She doubled herself," Dymitr says quietly.

All eyes swivel toward him, including Elza's. She shouldn't be surprised at this point. Dymitr has always been best at understanding the monsters' magic, at sensing it and tracing it and identifying it. He's the one who told her never to give her name, when she could help it, and who explained the missing teeth and fingernails on the fresh body they discovered, once, while tracing a rusałka through the plains south of here. *Teeth and fingernails are useful,* he said, as if she should have known it already.

So she wasn't surprised, the way Kazik was, when their grandmother made Dymitr curse-bearer, the keeper of a Knight's holy rituals. The rituals are like magic, and Dymitr understands magic.

Marzena's eyes glitter a little as she looks at her youngest son. "Yes, *she* did."

Until then she didn't realize that Dymitr called the strzyga "she," like it was a person. But that, too, is typical. It's what their grandmother said a few minutes ago: this is the flaw in Dymitr's heart that he must do penance to correct. And he has. Elza has never known a Knight to submit himself to more penance than Dymitr did in the months before he left for Chicago. Steeling himself for what was to come.

And despite how good his instincts are, Elza didn't trust him to do his mission alone. She's the reason he has to start over from scratch. She feels the ache of guilt, and wishes she'd apologized to him, instead of the other way around.

"There were two strzygas in that clearing," Marzena says. "One a mirror image of the other."

Ala prepares an illusion in her mind, like loading a gun: Dymitr, as he was this evening when he set out: dark pants, worn at the knee; a black shirt with the sleeves rolled up to his elbows, creased here and there from packing, and fraying at the cuffs. Dark circles under his eyes. His hair curling a little at the ends, too long.

Holding that image in her head, just in case, she slips out of Dymitr's room. In the hallway, it's easier to hear the hymns sung in reedy voices over the body, and the cold, urgent voice speaking over it.

"One a mirror image of the other," the voice says, and Ala's steps falter as she thinks for one horrible moment that she's been spotted, Dymitr's own mirror image prowling through the back of the house. But the voice continues.

"Time for you to go," Ala says, to the dybbuk on her back.

For a moment, she worries the dybbuk will break its promise, and keep clinging to her. But with a click of its teeth and a flutter of dark fabric, its weight lifts, and it disappears. She doesn't know where it will go, which of the Knight cousins it will attach itself to, but she hopes it chooses wisely.

It strikes her as a little funny, in a dark way. The Knights going to all this effort to keep a spirit from invading them, possessing them . . . but none of their rituals will prevent the dybbuk from doing just that.

"Mirroring is a strange sort of magic, beyond the capabilities of a strzyga, so it must have consulted a witch somewhere along its path." Marzena sits back in her chair. "After that, I matched the footprints that walked into the clearing with the set of tracks that walked out. I followed the strzyga back out of the forest to a little hotel close to the big road. But it was nowhere to be found. The hotel manager had seen it, though he didn't know what it really was, but he couldn't say where it had gone. So I did what I always do."

She looks at Łukasz, who's resting his chin on his hand, his elbow propped up next to a plate of bread.

"You paid the hotel manager off," he supplies, when prompted.

"I paid the hotel manager off," Marzena agrees. "He let me into the room the strzyga used and there, I found all

I needed." She reaches out and tugs at the young cousin's dark blond braid. "A strand of its hair."

At the end of the table, André gasps. At first Elza thinks it's just a reaction to the story—and a melodramatic one, at that. But André hunches over his plate, breathing hard. Krystyna puts an arm across his shoulders, speaking softly to him and touching a hand to his forehead.

"How did you find it with *hair*?" the cousin asks, pulling her braid free of Marzena's grasp. The question draws everyone's attention back to the story, to Marzena, as Krystyna ushers André into the kitchen.

"I didn't," Marzena says. "I called the dogs."

She tugs up her left sleeve, revealing a bandage down the length of her arm, from wrist to elbow. Elza has a similar wound on her own left arm, which she used to summon a murder of crows—at the time, she thought she was helping Dymitr escape a pack of strzygas, though now she knows she did more harm than good.

What Marzena summoned wasn't "dogs," of course, but wolves. A pack of them, with otherworldly strength and focus. Despite their size, they're easier to call forth than crows, which are faster and resist control by their very nature. Wolves are pack animals, used to following a single leader. Of all the Knights Elza knows, Marzena calls the strongest, most fully realized wolves. She has a way with dogs, their grandmother says. Always has.

"I offered the hair to the wolves, and they led me to the

strzyga. It was wounded, so it hadn't gone far. It was limping along the road." She tilts from side to side to mimic
the strzyga's gait. "It didn't even warrant the drawing of
my sword. I sent the wolves ahead of me, and watched
them overtake it. When they were finished with it, there
wasn't much left. Some entrails and some feathers."

She reaches into the inner pocket of her jacket, and
takes out a single feather. It's brown, and dotted with white
at regular intervals, like it was dabbed with paint. A pretty
little thing, to belong to such a monstrous creature as a
strzyga.

Elza sees Dymitr's hands in his lap, clenched so hard it
looks painful.

"We will bury my brother with this small trophy,"
Łukasz says, his voice solemn and quiet. "So he knows
that he's avenged."

Marzena adds, "And then you and I will finish what
he started, and pick off the rest of Athene's strzyga clan."

"Hear hear," Elza's grandmother says, thumping the table with a fist. Then she raises her wineglass to Marzena.
All around the table, everyone picks up their glasses, even
the young cousins, who have only kompot or apple juice.
As one, everyone drinks.

And then Marzena's spell is broken. A few others go
into the next room to join the singers who watch over
Filip's body. Marzena takes the feather in there with them,
to slide it into Filip's clasped hands, beneath the beads of

the rosary. Everyone else helps to clear the table of the dirty plates.

It's not until Elza is piling up the napkins that she realizes: she didn't see Dymitr toast their mother for her victory.

🌸

"When they were finished with it," Ala hears from the dining room, "there wasn't much left. Some entrails and some feathers."

A shiver crawls down Ala's spine. She hurries into the bathroom and closes the door behind her. Dymitr told her the book of curses was hidden under the bathroom sink. She opens the cabinet doors there and sees, in the back of the door, two names drawn on the wood in waxy crayon. On one side: ELZA. On the other side: DYMEK.

Under the sink, she finds a scrub brush and a bottle of bleach, a few spare rolls of toilet paper, a stack of washcloths. But Dymitr explained the hiding spot to her carefully: she has to feel along the cabinet's left side, because there's a false wall there. She feels it give way a little under the pressure of her fingers, and slides it to the side, expecting to run her fingers over the dark blue leather cover of the journal his grandmother handed to him in the memory.

She feels nothing.

Alarm prickles over the back of Ala's neck. She runs her fingers all along the cabinet wall. Then she taps along the false panel she slid back to see if the book got stuck there somehow. She uses her phone's flashlight to peer inside the cabinet itself, moving the washcloths to the side, feeling along the pipes, knocking over the stack of toilet paper rolls.

There's nothing. The book isn't there.

And there are footsteps coming right toward her.

A SONG FOR THE DEAD

The next song is "Zegar bije, wspominaj na ostatnie rzeczy," and Elza feels the familiar tune prickling over the back of her neck. *The clock is ticking,* the droning voices from the living room say to her, *remember the last things.*

She remembers the last time Filip spoke to her—doubling back to the house before he left on this mission that brought him only death, he asked her if she'd seen his wallet. She rolled her eyes and reached into his left jacket pocket to produce it. "You know me best," he said to her. "More a teacher than a student from the start."

Remember the last things, she thinks, and she leaves the chaos of the kitchen to get just a moment alone. She walks down the narrow hallway and around the corner to the part of the house she shared with Dymitr and Kazik, growing up. After Kazik moved out, it was just her and Dymitr, their doors facing each other, a cramped bathroom perpendicular to them both.

She steps into her room and runs her hands over the clothes in her closet without turning on the light. She feels scratchy tulle and stiff brocade and soft cashmere and sturdy wool. She lets a tear fall, and then another, thinking of the lonely clearing in the woods where Filip fell, owl feathers all around; and thinking of sitting across the chessboard from him as he bit down on the top of a pawn—he was always chewing while thinking, her uncle Filip.

She hears a creak in the hallway outside, and says, "Dymek?" And she wipes her cheeks and nudges her bedroom door open with the toe of her boot. Sure enough, Dymitr is standing in his bedroom.

"Got tired of washing up?" she says to him.

"Just needed a break," he says. "You?"

His tone is off. Gruff. Like he's angry about something. She wonders if it's the same thing that's making her angry.

"I hate funerals," she says. "I know, I know—who likes them? But I *really* hate them."

Another tear falls, and she hardly feels it. She leans into her doorframe, and he leans into his, so they're across from each other.

"Do you ever think . . ." His brow furrows in a way that looks new to her, though she's seen every expression his face is capable of. "Do you ever think about what sort of people we are, that we celebrate a murder like this?"

It takes her a moment to understand. They're not here to celebrate, after all. But maybe that's how it feels to him—like a feast. So she nods. "No one has shed a tear for him. He was murdered by a monster and all we do is cheer about the monster being dead."

His face is passive.

"I know, I know," she says. "You don't like when I call them monsters. You never have."

A twitch of a smile. "I suppose I prefer specificity."

"You prefer compassion, even when you have to repent of it."

"Repent of it." He looks a little startled.

"Don't tell me all those hours of penance have slipped from your memory."

"No, no. Of course not." His smile doesn't quite spread to his eyes.

Unease surges inside her like the swell of a wave. She's been dismissing Dymitr's odd behavior all night. His fearful expression as he listened to Marzena's story, his insistence on calling the strzyga "she," and now this.

"Did something happen in Chicago?" she says.

"No. Why?"

"No reason." She smiles. "Hold on, I need some lip balm."

She steps back into her dark bedroom and fumbles in the drawer of her bedside table, keeping an eye on the hallway. As she pretends to search the drawer with one hand, she curls her fingers into her palm with the other, her fingernails cutting into the skin. Knight magic floods her body, hot and prickling, and she looks back at Dymitr, her heart racing.

But there's no strangeness in him, no shadow. Just her brother.

She lets the magic fade before she goes back into the hallway.

"Do you remember our hiding place?" he asks her.

It's the feeling of their names drawn on the cabinet door that comes to mind first. DYMEK on one side, ELZA on the other, scribbled on the wood in crayon. If their parents—or even their grandmother—had found out about it, they would have both been punished for the defacing, but no one ever had, not even Kazik.

It was how they passed notes, even after they had both started their training as Knights. Maybe especially then. Because complaining wasn't allowed, and the punishment for it was too severe to risk anyone overhearing, so their best chance at an honest conversation was to write it down, fold it up small, and tuck it into the corner of the bathroom cabinet, just above the bottle of bleach.

"Under the sink? How could I forget?"

"I just wondered if you'd checked it recently."

She feels suddenly aware of her heartbeat. "Why, did you leave me something?"

Before he can answer, she hears the sound of broken glass in the kitchen, and trades an alarmed look with him. She walks down the hallway to see what broke, and finds one of the vases of chrysanthemums shattered on the floor, the water spreading out from the point of impact, and the flowers scattered everywhere.

And on his knees, picking up the biggest pieces of glass one by one . . . is Dymitr.

Elza looks over her shoulder, but she doesn't see the Dymitr she was just speaking to behind her. She thinks of the strzyga mirroring herself with magic. Her breaths come faster and shallower, but her mind is quiet. She walks across the kitchen, sidestepping the young cousins and walking into the room where Filip's body waits with a feather and a rosary tucked into his palms.

She touches her grandmother's elbow to get her attention.

And at that moment, the front door opens for a second time that evening. The singers, Krystyna included, falter in their hymn for just a moment, and her grandmother gestures for them to continue. Kazik steps into the house, breathless, and says:

"A wieszczy! A wieszczy at the burial plot."

Elza's grandmother straightens, becoming Joanna Myśliwiec all at once.

"All the Knights except Marzena and I will search," she says to him. "All the rest will stay and sing."

"You don't think I'll be an asset to the search party?" Marzena demands hotly.

"I think you'll be an asset in protecting Filip's body and the vulnerable people who remain behind," Joanna replies.

"Babcia," Elza says.

"We can't allow that *thing* to pollute Filip's grave."

"Babcia!" Elza is surprised by the force of her own voice. Joanna turns toward her, her mouth in a thin line, the way she looks when she's about to scold someone. But she must see the urgency in Elza's eyes, because she doesn't scold, she only waits.

"I have to tell you something, too," Elza says. "Right now."

She thinks of the old hymn.

The clock is ticking.

Hell is opening.

A TENSE CONVERSATION

The house is in chaos, and Dymitr feels sick to his stomach. Marzena's words are pounding like a headache. *It,* she called the strzyga. *It didn't even warrant the drawing of my sword.*

He tries to go through the motions of cleaning the kitchen with the others, but the words chase him. *I sent the wolves ahead of me, and watched them overtake it.* He doesn't flinch when the vase breaks, just kneels to pick up the pieces.

André is sitting on a stool in the corner, a wet rag on his head. He got faint during dinner, but he doesn't look like he's about to pass out now—if anything, he looks more focused than usual, staring at Dymitr as he puts the shards of the vase into a dish towel.

"Feeling okay?" he asks his young cousin.

"Never better," the boy replies, in a deep voice that doesn't quite belong to him.

Before he can puzzle over this, though, Kazik comes back to warn them of the wieszczy, and Dymitr's stomach lurches. It can't be a coincidence. This must be Niko's doing. A well-timed distraction designed to sow chaos among the Knights.

Whatever Niko is planning, it's happening *now*.

When they were finished with it, there wasn't much left.

Some entrails and some feathers.

All he wants is to stay behind while the search party looks for the wieszczy that may or may not be Niko's accomplice; all he wants is to stay here and clean the kitchen and pretend that he doesn't come from a family full of gleeful, righteous murderers. But he knows what he has to do: he has to go out there with the others and try to find the wieszczy before any of them do, to warn it away. No small feat, since he's far from the best tracker among them.

He puts on his boots. The front door is open, letting in the night air. Two reedy voices sing in the living room, keeping up their determined vigil even while the rest of the house prepares for battle. When he straightens, his grandmother is standing in front of him, Marzena lingering behind her.

"Go to the weapons room with Marzena," she says. "She and I need to tell you something before you go out with the rest."

There's only one possible response to an order like that, especially with his mother watching: "Yes, Babcia."

The weapons room is in the back of the house, separated from the living quarters by a small courtyard. Technically, a hallway connects the front of the house to the back, but it may as well be a covered walkway. It's never had glass in the windows in all the time he's lived here, and its stone floor makes it cold even in summer.

A chill passes over him as he follows his mother down it, observing the overgrown greenery in the courtyard that no one can be bothered to tend, the statue of an angel holding a horn. Dymitr looked it up once and found out that it was Saint Michael, the leader of the army of heaven, holding the symbol of Świętowit, the Slavic god of war. Someone had even attached a—real, sharp—dagger against the statue's spine, as if he was a Knight.

Knights of the Holy Order take all symbols as their own, even if it's blasphemy.

Marzena opens the door to the weapons room, which is all stone and heavy wood, with no windows. Weapons line the walls, and heavy cabinets against the far wall hold the other gear—armor, mostly. His mother ushers him in, and he looks at the bench that Filip sat on to remove his bloody boots, a pew taken from an old church.

The memory catches him in its current, for a moment. He thinks of Filip handing his younger self the bloody boots, as if it was normal to let a child scrub gore from your shoes after you'd returned from a murder.

Every memory he has here is a horror, even the good ones.

He hears his grandmother's footsteps behind him, recognizable because of their halting rhythm. She's holding a sword, and that's not strange, because she's about to go out hunting, and her spine sword has been too difficult for her to draw for years now.

But then Elza steps into the room, followed by . . . him.

Dymitr is looking at an exact copy of himself. Black trousers, black shirt with the sleeves rolled up to his elbows. Scarred lip. Pale cheek. Scuffs on his shoes. It's like he's looking into a mirror, only his reflection is moving, and he's completely still.

The other Dymitr is staring wide-eyed at Joanna like she's a particularly terrifying beast he's never encountered before. The smell of him is rich and dark. *We can't read emotions that aren't fear,* Ala told him, in one of their many lessons. *But sometimes we can make sense of what the fear is woven together with.*

In this case, the fear is bitter with rage.

"So you see," Joanna says, pointing to the exact replica of Dymitr standing across from him, "why we have a problem."

Then Marzena is closing the door behind them, and dragging the bolt across it. Locking them all in together.

He doesn't dare speak. He knows that the person standing across from him must be Ala, with such a strong illusion layered over her that he can't see behind it. It takes incredible skill and strength to project an illusion so sturdy and so perfect—and so detailed, because even the folds of their sleeves match exactly. He would marvel at it if he wasn't so terrified by it. Ala came here to help him. She came here, and now she's a zmora locked in the weapons room with three Knights.

She's going to die if he doesn't convince them to release her.

"I—" he begins.

"Shut up," his grandmother says. "I don't need you to speak to identify which one of you is real and which one isn't."

She steps into the circle of light cast by the fixture above his head, the creases in her face even more pronounced because of its harshness. He watches, frozen with horror, as she drags the sword's edge against the meat of her palm, just enough to draw blood. Her eyes turn deep crimson.

Even if he was capable of producing an illusion to rival Ala's, he wouldn't try. The only way to get her out of here safely is to pretend not to be himself. He's helpless beneath his grandmother's stare. She looks at him, and then at Ala, and he prays her illusion holds up to a Knight's scrutiny.

His grandmother turns back to him.

"Did you think I wouldn't notice a zmora right under my nose?" she demands, and then she swings the sword, striking him in the side of the head with the hilt.

Everything goes dark and hazy for a moment, and he has to put a hand on the floor to steady himself. He tastes dark chocolate in the back of his throat, and lifts his eyes to Ala's—to his own.

"Now that we've resolved that issue," Ala says coolly, "I should go search for the other one."

He holds his throbbing head. She sounds just like him, which must be part of the illusion, too. He wonders, though, if this is how she hears him. If he sounds this . . . hard. Businesslike.

"The other one?" Joanna demands.

"I suspect I was pursued here by the zmora and the strzygoń I deceived in Chicago." Ala looks at Elza using Dymitr's eyes, Dymitr's face. "You know who I mean. You're the one who revealed my true nature to them, after all."

Elza looks away, her cheeks pink.

"I did," she says, after a moment. "Which one do you think *that* is?"

She points at Dymitr. He doesn't dare speak—doesn't dare *move*—until Ala is safely out of this room.

"Hard to say," Ala replies. "That could be a zmora projecting a strong illusion. Or it could be a strzygoń altered by magic. I'll go search for the other one—it can't be far, they've been moving in a pair."

Joanna nods. "Elza, go keep watch on the house while Dymitr searches. Marzena and I will stay here and question it."

Ala looks at Dymitr. He sees nothing of the real her in the eyes of the illusion. She looks at him like he's less than nothing.

"Just don't kill it, please, Babcia," she says. "It knows too much about me, and I'd like to find out how."

She slides the bolt away from the door, and walks out of

the room with Elza at her heels. No one stops her. Dymitr sags with relief.

Ala is out. Ala is safe.

🦁

Dymitr was afraid of the book of curses for a long time. Joanna gave it to him the day before he became a Knight, so there was a lot to distract him—namely, the splitting of his soul, a procedure that was outlined in the pages of the very book he sought to avoid. So he brought it back to his room and set it on the desk and tried to forget about it.

But after the agony of transformation was past, he was still the curse-bearer, the one entrusted with the Knights' magic. He couldn't avoid the book forever. So one evening he made himself sit down and read it cover to cover.

It contained all the things he expected: the magic of the bone sword, the incantations for summoning deadly crows and wolves, the instructions for tethering a pack of upiór to your will. But it also had things he would never have dreamed of: bloodline curses to eradicate entire family lines, like the one that almost killed Ala; spells to take a creature's senses, or addle their thoughts, or rob them of their magic; and worst of all, an entire section for torments.

They were in no particular order. Spells for the skin, to shrink, or harden, or split, or burn. Spells for bones, to break, bend, twist, and shatter. Spells for the heart, to race or slow or to change its rhythm. But worst of the worst were the spells for the mind: to convince it of falsehoods, like that the body was being devoured by a clew of flesh-eating worms, or that the tormentor was a member of the victim's family, inflicting harm for no reason; or to control its thoughts, bringing forth old horrors again and again, or erasing pleasant memories so that only sorrow was left, or inducing panic, paranoia, hysteria, hallucinations, rage.

A Knight's magic came from pain, but pain took on new meaning as he flipped through the pages of the book of curses, discovering new sensations you could force a mind to conjure—to feel more, to feel less, to feel wrong.

So he knows what to fear when his mother grabs him by the hair and slams his forehead into the stone floor, knows what awaits him when his grandmother kneels on his spine and binds his hands behind him.

And he begs, accordingly.

"Please," he says. "Please, have mercy—"

He can't insist on his true identity now. Ala got out, but the only reason they're not hunting her down is that they think she's the real him. And besides—what would they do, if they knew the truth? They would kill him anyway, for being a zmora.

Her voice is harsh and hard. "There is a wieszczy in town. I am not a fool; I know a distraction when I see one. So what is the wieszczy intended to distract us from?"

He has no answer. She kicks him in the side. Her boots are heavy and she has the strength of a Knight; he curls in on himself, his ribs shrieking with pain.

Dymitr tastes blood. "I have nothing to do with the wieszczy—"

His grandmother brings the back of her hand down on his face so hard that he sprawls with his hands bound behind him.

"I do not believe in coincidence," his grandmother says, so quietly he has to strain to hear her. "I wish to know what you're planning. I wish to know how you were able to pass among us so easily, what magic you did to learn so much about my grandson. And I wish to know how many of you there are. You may begin with the latter, since that question is simplest."

He looks up at her from the corner of his eye.

"I'm alone," he says.

"Liar," she replies.

Marzena crouches beside him, and presses her knee into his throat so hard he can't breathe, let alone speak.

"Do you want to do it, or should I?" Marzena says to his grandmother.

"I'll do it," his grandmother says, and Dymitr struggles against his mother's hold, his body thrashing like he's a fish on a dock struggling back toward water. But Marzena is strong, and Joanna kneels on one of his legs, then presses him down with her full weight.

His vision is going dark at the edges when his grandmother rolls up her sleeve to her elbow and starts dragging the edge of the blade across her forearm, making short but deep cuts that bleed rich red.

"Tenfold hurt, tenfold lasting," she says in a low whisper. "Ten times given and ten times spoken. Ten by ten what's suffered must be . . . tenfold felt what's tenfold broken."

He recognizes the spell from the book of curses. *Amplificare* was written beside it. A pain amplification spell, to intensify his physical pain by a factor of ten.

He can smell it when it settles over him. Copper, that's the odor of Knight magic. It smells like blood and like sickness, like wrongness. He wonders how he could have missed it, before; he remembers that he could never smell it, before. And then he feels the rough stone digging into his skin, and the ache in his ribs and in his cheek intensifies so much he lets out a loud, desperate sob of pain.

The pressure of his mother's knee lets up on his throat, but he can still feel her—and smell her—behind him. His grandmother stands.

"Let's begin," she says.

Marzena draws the knife from her boot, and grabs him by the hair again to drag him upright. He has to bite back a scream at the pulling in his scalp, which feels like she's trying to rip off his skin. His eyes are full of tears, though he's never cried from pain before, not even when he was strapped face down at his Knight ceremony and his grandmother was cutting a line across his shoulders to create space for the bone sword.

"What," his grandmother says, her mouth twisted into a sneer, "are you planning?"

"I can't—" He chokes. He's already in so much pain, and they're only just beginning. "I can't tell you—"

Pain explodes across his back as Marzena drags her knife over his shoulder blade.

He screams.

A SCREAM IN THE NIGHT

Ala never thought of herself as steady in a crisis until her mother, deteriorating rapidly thanks to the bloodline curse that later passed to Ala herself, begged for death, and Ala granted it.

Ala looked at her bone-pale, emaciated mother, shuddering in the corner of her bathroom, and opened the medicine cabinet to tip a few sleeping pills into her hand. Just enough to ferry her mother into unconsciousness. She ran her hand over her mother's hair as the woman drank them down with the glass of water from her bedside table.

Then, once she drifted off, Ala found the sharpest blade in the house to take care of the rest. She remembers only select moments from the act itself—how warm her mother's skin was against her hand as she eased her down into a prone position on the tile, how hard it was to actually pierce her flesh—

But the aftermath is a stain she can't remove from her mind. There was so much blood.

She accomplished it all without weeping, without hysterics, and without hesitation. Even Klara commented on it when she came to collect the body so that the Dry-jas could dispose of it for her. Ala was just sitting on the couch in her living room, watching *Law & Order,* her mother's corpse wrapped in a dark sheet on the bathroom floor. Everything was neat and tidy. Even Ala's fingernails were trim and clean. Klara said, *It's a little disturbing how calm you are, you know.*

Ala kept waiting for the breakdown after that, for the moment when the numbness faded and the horror set in. But there was less horror than she expected in the act of releasing her mother from agony.

※

She didn't panic back then, and she doesn't panic now, moving through the trees in pursuit of Nikodem Kostka. He can't have gone far. His quarry—Marzena, Dymitr's mother—is still inside.

The sight of Marzena, with just enough of Dymitr in her eyes and in her mouth to make the comparison un-avoidable, watching impassively as Joanna bashed the hilt of her sword into her son's head, made Ala feel like she'd been caught in a winter rain and drenched to the bone.

And Joanna herself—so *familiar* in a way she hadn't been when Ala walked through one of Dymitr's memo-ries. Her mind was too addled by the fear of the curse to really pay attention, then, but in person, Joanna's eyes, her *face*—

It's better not to think of that now. If she thinks of what

she saw in that weapons room, then she'll think of Dymitr with his mouth determinedly closed, letting her pretend to be him to save her own skin even though it means pain and death for him.

All her doubts about Dymitr's new loyalties are gone now. And she's equally sure that he'll forgive her for ridding herself of the torments his grandmother caused her. Of all the people that walk the earth, she's the only one he won't be able to condemn for killing one of his family.

Not after he killed one of hers.

Her nose isn't impressive by zmora standards, but it's not difficult to pick out Niko from the smell of wet earth and car exhaust permeating the woods. He smells like anxiety and trepidation, like powdered sugar and hazelnut. Ala's mouth waters as she follows the scent to its source.

He's crouched at the edge of the woods, near the back of the house but still in position to watch the front door. When she draws near, his hand moves to the hilt of the knife at his side. His bright eyes fix on her, and he relaxes.

"I need your help," she says, and maybe she's not as calm and steady as she thinks, because he comes to his feet, looking alarmed.

"What happened?"

"After I let the dybbuk loose, I . . . ran into someone. Dymitr's sister. I had an illusion at the ready, but she saw two of us. Two Dymitrs." She fights to swallow. "I couldn't get away. I convinced them I was him, but now they have him instead—and they know he's a zmora."

A scream—distant but agonized—sounds from somewhere deep in the house, like the house is a ship and the scream is its horn, wailing into the night as a warning to fellow travelers. She feels it in every inch of her body, and she knows it's Dymitr.

Niko's face flickers into his owl form in the space of a moment: he's a man, then a sharp-beaked bird with wings manifesting over his shoulders, and then a man again, knife drawn, eyes wild.

"Fucking hell, I have to go in there," Niko says. "I have to get him, I have to—"

Ala, though, feels the steadiness of knowing what she needs to do, even if it's dangerous, even if it will kill her.

"I have a plan," she says. "And it's very, very stupid."

16

A PERFECT REFLECTION

Ordinarily, for a transformation like this, Niko would make a detailed plan. He would research the area and choose the right place for a moderate work of magic, a place bought at a price by people who loved it. It's a difficult task in Poland, not because there aren't enough suitable places, but because it's too soaked in pain. Six million Polish people died here in the Second World War alone, half of them Jewish, and he would never dare to draw magic from the sites of deep horror where those lives were lost, death camps and bloody battles. But even if he did, the magic wouldn't cooperate. It would bend back on itself. That's the nature of magic that comes from pain. It's why the Holy Order's magic can only ever harm.

So ordinarily, he would find a building that took a long time to build—or rebuild, in the aftermath of the war. He would pick the lock in the dead of night, when he's unlikely to be disturbed. And he would kneel there to draw the magic from the ground.

Ordinarily, that's how he would do it.

There's no time for that now. He goes to the first place

he can think of, which is the shore of the pond where the dybbuk attacked him. The dybbuk took a risk by releasing that girl from its hold, and that act of sacrifice makes it as good a place as any for the kind of magic he needs to do. He doesn't see the girl anywhere, and he's glad. It means she woke, and will find her way back to civilization.

He kneels in the mud, and tucks one of Ala's buttons—plucked from the cuff of her shirt—into his fist before plunging his hands into the pond.

He can feel the magic here, humming in the water. It's as if an electric current is passing through it, prickling over his fingers. He takes a deep breath.

"Chciałbym przybrać inną formę," he says, "aby dokonać zemsty."

I wish to take another shape, for the purpose of revenge.

There are three methods for performing spoken magic. It can be commanded, as he did to transform Dymitr's pulled fingernail into pure light. It can be caught in the net of a riddle or a rhyme and dragged into being. And it can be requested. The first is the fastest method, good for quick, small acts that don't require a lot of power. But you have to be in control of the debt that invites magic in—you have to have something to offer, a name or an act or a gift, or the magic will backfire. The second—catching magic in a rhyme—is the most powerful, but if the rhyme's net isn't strong enough, the magic will twist away from you. And the third method—asking—depends on whether the magic of the place is sympathetic to the request. He thinks the magic of the dybbuk will be sympathetic to his desire to fight Knights, but he's not sure. Maybe revenge is not righteous enough for it.

He waits with his hands in the water as the magic decides. That's how he thinks of it, anyway, as slight currents pass over his knuckles and work their way over the veins of his hands. Testing him, maybe, or maybe that's just the most sense he can make of something that isn't sensible. Magic is wild, as Baba Jaga often reminds him, and it resists feeble attempts to master it, so it's best not to try unless you're sure of your own power. She is maybe the only person alive who truly controls magic, and even she finds it wriggling away from her sometimes.

As the magic sparks over his hands, he thinks to add a simple: "Proszę."

It's that *please* that does it, he thinks. He feels the currents working their way between his fingers to wrap around the button in his fist. He opens his hand, and lets the button fall to the pond's muddy bottom.

A black tendril, hair fine, creeps across the back of his hand and over his wrist. As he watches, it spreads over his skin in a web of black, multiplying again and again. He's reminded of a time when, as a child, he punctured a spider's egg sac with a needle, and hundreds of baby spiders spread from the punctured hole at once. The blackness crawls up his arms and disappears beneath his sleeves, but he can still feel it, like thousands of crawling feet racing over his skin.

The sensation is revolting, but Niko stays still, letting the magic do its work. He closes his eyes when the dark tendrils creep over his cheeks and nose, and he can feel his body shifting beneath his clothes. He's shrinking, the fabric falling heavier against his skin. Then he feels pressure against his bones, like two hands pushing inward on his shoulders, and then pulling outward at his hips. He bites down on a scream.

But the magic is gentle, all things considered. When he opens his eyes, he finds narrow fingers and delicate wrists, small breasts and a bend in his waist, muscled thighs straining against pants not quite built for them. He takes his hands from the water and probes at his high cheekbones and the thin lines of hair above his eyes.

He's wearing Ala's body.

"Well that was unnerving," Ala herself says, stepping out of the woods. "Keep your hands to yourself, would you?"

"You know, I see women all the time and manage to keep my hands off them," he says, in a higher, clearer voice than his own. "I think I can handle it now, too."

He stands, and his pants sag, so he hoists them up to his new waist and pulls the belt tighter. Then he rolls up his pant legs so they're not dragging on the ground. There's not much he can do about the oversized shirt except tie it at the bottom.

He's too frantic to dwell on the strange feeling of being smaller and differently shaped than he was two minutes ago. He feels like there's a hand tugging him back toward the house where Dymitr is being tortured by people who claim to love him.

But they don't love him, Niko thinks. Because if love doesn't allow change, then what the fuck is that love worth?

He and Ala walk quickly through the woods. Once the house is in view, Ala stops to concentrate on her illusion. She has to appear as Dymitr again.

He's never met a zmora so talented with illusions before. Oh, there are powerful illusionists among the Dryjas, those who can put you in a different place entirely, who can make it feel and sound convincing. But the detail of Ala's constructions and the number of people she can project them to at once—it's something he would marvel at, if he didn't feel alarm prickling at his skin.

"You need to calm down," Ala says to him, her eyes closed. "I can't concentrate with you scared like this, it's like you're waterboarding me with hot chocolate."

"Sorry," Niko says.

She opens her eyes, and suddenly, she's Dymitr. Solemn gray eyes. Scarred lip. Stern brow. That look in his eyes, like he's always waiting for something.

He grabs Niko's wrist, and Niko almost falls against him with relief, almost reaches for his hand. But this isn't Dymitr, as convincing an illusion as it is, and Ala is only trying to bind Niko's wrists so he looks like a convincing prisoner. Niko puts his wrists together, and she ties them loosely with a length of rope he created from a strand of her hair—commanding magic, that time. It won't be difficult for him to pull his hands free, when the moment is right.

"Let's go," Ala says, in Dymitr's voice.

Niko nods, and they march toward the house, Ala with her hand firm on Niko's elbow, Niko stumbling alongside her, as if he's injured. Mud turns to gravel beneath his feet, and Ala puts one hand on the back of his neck as she pushes him up the front steps and through the front door.

The smell of bread and sour cake assaults his nose, and he hears two reedy voices singing a hymn in the next room. He doesn't look around—doesn't dare to, not in this place when he's supposed to be acting cowed and terrified. But he sees the old tile floors and the white lacy tablecloths and an old gramophone—Knights, too, are long-lived, and they bring the past with them wherever they go, just as Niko's people do.

Elza is there right away, her hand reaching back toward her spine—it's a Knight's reflex, she's ready to draw her bone swords. Her eyes are wide and alarmed as she takes in Niko's Ala-shaped face. She recognizes him. Her. Whatever.

"Why didn't you take her through the back?" Elza demands of Ala.

"I didn't want to waste time. Stay at your post," Ala replies. If Niko was asked to critique, he would say she sounds a little *too* much like a soldier barking orders at an underling, but Elza seems to accept it.

Ala steers Niko roughly toward the back of the house. He plays up his limp.

Just past the kitchen, they walk down a hallway lined with portraits. Each one is a photograph—some black-and-white, some color—of a fallen Knight. Niko scans them to see if anyone he's exacted vengeance on as zemsta is among them; he recognizes none of them, though he sees hints of Dymitr in them. A nose, a chin, and in more than one of them, a pair of gray eyes.

They walk past a courtyard where a statue of Michael the Archangel stands untended, a dagger glinting on its weather-worn back, and that's when he hears another sound—not a scream, because the time for screaming has passed. Screaming is for the first moments of pain, the shocking ones, the ones that happen before pain is so layered over itself that there's no energy left to scream.

No, what he hears is worse—it's a moan, a sob, a helpless, pathetic sound that rips out his insides.

Ala shows no recognition of it, but her hand tightens on his arm. She releases him and pounds on the door with her fist.

"Babcia!" she calls out. "I caught one!"

⚔

At the sight of Dymitr on the floor, Niko lets out a harsh breath.

It's only been twenty minutes since Ala found Niko in

the woods to ask for his help. But it seems that twenty minutes is plenty of time for Knights to do some damage.

Dymitr's back is soaked with blood. His black shirt is wet and sticking to him. His nose is bleeding, too, and one of his eyes is bloodshot. Swollen. Swollen eye, swollen lip. He's curled in on himself—to protect his internal organs, maybe. Or just like a dead leaf, curling up as it dries.

For a horrible moment Niko thinks maybe he *is* dead— but then he sees Dymitr's chest heaving, and gray eyes— hollowed out like the shell of a walnut—swivel to meet his.

Niko strains against Ala's hold, his body struggling toward Dymitr—but that's all right, because they think Dymitr is a strzygoń in disguise, and they think Niko is the zmora in cahoots with him. The old woman is scrutinizing him with the bright red eyes of a half-transformed Knight, but the younger one smirks at him, and he realizes she looks familiar. She looks like Dymitr.

This is his quarry.

Brzytwa. The Razor.

He's used to sizing up opponents before attacking them, used to watching them move and making quick assessments. As Marzena rises to her feet, her body uncoiling, he feels every one of his muscles tense in anticipation. She moves like a predator. He sees the flap in her boot that conceals a knife, the one Dymitr warned him about. He sees the bright red blood of her son on her palms.

"That one's a zmora. The female," Elza's voice says from the doorway. She followed them here. She nods to Niko, who she must recognize as Ala, from their confrontation on the street outside the Uptown Theatre. He feels the sudden urge to laugh as he realizes he's in yet another Shakespearean nightmare—switched bodies, switched identities, a night of confusion in the woods.

Elza adds: "So the one you captured earlier must be the strzygoń, disguised by magic. He's the stronger fighter."

"Perhaps it was," Marzena says, drawling a little. She nudges Dymitr hard with the toe of her boot, and Dymitr bites back a whimper. "Not in its current condition, I think."

"We'll use them against each other," Joanna says, as if it's already decided—and perhaps if she says it, it is. "I will take *that* one out—" She nods to Dymitr, still lying at her feet. "And question it further. It hardly poses a threat anymore. Marzena and Dymitr will handle this new one."

Niko's chest leaps with panic. He can't let Joanna drag the real Dymitr out of this room alone, to take him God knows where and do God knows *what* to him. Ala squeezes his arm.

"If you don't mind, Babcia, I'd like to speak to that one myself." Ala points at the real Dymitr, bleeding on the stone. "Since he's wearing my face and seems to know so much about me."

"Of course," Joanna says, and she smiles at Marzena. "I think your mother can handle one zmora on her own."

Marzena's eyes glitter as she looks Niko over, her eyes pausing on the belt cinching his too-large pants around his waist, the bob of his—or Ala's—throat as he swallows.

"Pick it up, if you would. It's been cursed with tenfold pain, so it may scream," Joanna says to Ala, and Ala moves toward Dymitr to obey. It's a strange sight, one Dymitr moving closer to another, like Ala stepped across a mirror and into the land of reflections. Niko tenses as she grabs Dymitr by the arm, hoping that she handles him gently and hoping that she remembers to be rough with him all at the same time.

Ala has a stronger stomach than he does. She wrenches Dymitr upright, and his jaw clenches around a moan, his swollen, bloodied face shiny with sweat and maybe tears, though it's hard to say. He stumbles to his feet, and Ala pays him no mind, half marching and half dragging him toward the door. Elza opens it for them both, and as Dymitr stumbles past his sister, she spits on him, hitting him in the cheek.

Then Joanna, Elza, Dymitr, and Ala walk out of the room, Ala still wearing Dymitr's face like a veil.

And Nikodem Kostka, the Kostka zemsta, is alone with the Razor.

A FEINT

Ala's jaw aches as she half carries, half drags Dymitr into the hallway beyond the weapons room. The drone of the empty night singers across the house reminds her of cicadas in summer. The hallway is lit by moonlight, blue-gray and bare. She breathes in through her nose, and tastes the dark chocolate of Dymitr's terror on her tongue, but nothing from the woman he calls Babcia except the powder sweet of anxiety.

Maybe it's nice, Ala thinks, to live with so little fear. But it makes Joanna Myśliwiec stranger to her than any so-called monster that walks the earth.

Ala feels a different kind of fear, though. Anticipation. Apprehension. She feels the itching in her fingers that drives her to draw the knife at her back and stab Joanna Myśliwiec in the side. She feels her mother's flesh giving way to the knife that ended her pain. She remembers how it feels to deliver death, and she dreads it, and she craves it.

The end of her nightmares is at hand. Just a few minutes more.

"In here," Joanna says, and she leads the way into the

courtyard where the statue of the Archangel Michael stands, worn by weather and surrounded by untamed weeds. Ala takes note of the dagger sheathed at the small of Joanna's back; she wishes she could disarm her right now, but she doesn't want to give herself away before she has Joanna trapped.

It's a relief to be outside, even if they are surrounded on all sides by walls. The earth is soft beneath Ala's shoes, and she feels the weight of the knife she borrowed against her shoulder. She shoves Dymitr into the courtyard, still playing her part, and her teeth squeak from grinding when he makes one of those horrible, agonized sounds. She closes the door behind her, and locks it.

It feels a little like locking herself in a room with a grizzly.

Earlier, Joanna's voice threatened to launch Ala into the past. In the memory she'd once shared with Dymitr, Joanna was speaking to her grandson, and she did it at a higher pitch, with a gentler timbre. But in the weapons room, when she addressed him no longer believing he could possibly be her grandson, it was with a cold cruelty that Ala recognized from the vision of the zmora. *She hit me. I think she should lose the hand she used before she dies.*

In the weapons room, Ala stuffed the memory down. But now, she lets it come. She lets herself see the desperate zmora turning into animal after animal, as if the illusions could help her escape. She lets herself watch the Knight pin the zmora's wrist to the ground.

Her eyes are full of tears. The image that lingers, more than the stringy hair clinging to the zmora's lips or the firm hands of the male Knight pressing her to the earth, is the light in young Joanna's eyes as she moves her sword back and forth over the zmora's flesh. She can't decide, even now, if it's delight or determination.

Ala blinks the tears away, but she can hear them in her voice—in Dymitr's voice—when she speaks next.

"Do you ever feel for them?" she asks, feeling distant from the whole scene—from Dymitr sagging on his knees by the door where she set him down, his back flayed and blood dribbling from his mouth; from the nettle and mugwort and mustard growing in the untended courtyard, tangled around the base of the Saint Michael statue; from Joanna Myśliwiec, older than the fervent Knight of Ala's cursed recollections but no less brutal, standing across from her.

"What?" Joanna asks her, as if she misheard. "Do *you* feel bad for this thing wearing your face?"

"Don't you?" Ala tilts her head. "He looks like me, after all. What if we're wrong, and he's just a zmora with a skill for illusions? Doesn't it pain you to hurt someone who looks just like your grandson?"

"It doesn't," she says, and Ala believes her. "Other Knights will tell you that zmoras are benign, that a strzyga is a much more impressive kill—but those Knights are fools. The first zmora I hunted made me see visions of my father burning alive. The second zmora I hunted made me feel insects burrowing into my skin. They can make you see things that aren't there, hear things that never were, feel things that no one should ever have to feel."

Her voice has gone low and guttural, like it was in the memory Ala wishes she didn't have, and for the first time she wonders if Joanna is scarred by the creatures she's killed, even though she has no right to be. Trauma doesn't ask whether the person experiencing it is a sympathetic figure or not, after all.

"Foul things they are, among the most wretched of the monsters we hunt," Joanna continues. "A curse upon the earth that it is our duty to obliterate. But not to be underestimated."

"You hunted them," Ala says. "*You* hunted *them,* and they did what they could to survive you, but you call them 'foul'?"

Joanna regards her in silence for a long moment.

"Who are you?" she asks, casually, as if she's asking how cold it will be today so she can choose the right jacket.

Letting go of the illusion feels like unclenching a fist. Ala releases it, becoming herself again, and for the first time, stands face-to-face with the woman who cursed her family.

She can hear it again, what Joanna said when she passed the book of curses to Dymitr for safekeeping. *With this book, I can not only summon stronger weapons to fight my enemies—I can make those fights unnecessary.* Joanna's intention was to avoid this very confrontation—to kill off Ala's entire family, one by one, without ever having to look Ala in the eye or even become aware of her existence.

Well, Ala thinks, *too damn bad.*

"Someone you cursed," Ala says, her voice trembling with rage. She drew her knife—more of a short sword, really—without realizing it, and she's holding it with the blade tilted up, ready.

Joanna cocks her head, her silver hair catching the moonlight. "Did I, now."

"I don't know how far back it went," Ala says. "The first person I heard about was my aunt. Then my cousin. Then my mother. Then me."

"Then it did its job," Joanna says passively. "Though it has not, I see, finished that job with you quite yet. Are you here to exact your revenge before you die?"

"Oh, I'm cured," Ala says, with a forced grin. "Thanks to your grandson."

She smells something sweet as peach nectar. She's finally succeeded in making Joanna afraid, though she doesn't know exactly why, or exactly how. She thinks it's the fear that a person feels when they know something is true but don't want to admit it to themselves. She thinks it's something like dread.

"You're lying," Joanna says.

"Am I?" Ala raises her eyebrows. "Or did you lose your grip on your beloved curse-bearer?"

Before Joanna can respond, Ala lunges with the knife outstretched. She thought, in this moment, she would be half-hearted—not accustomed to killing, maybe she wouldn't be able to strike as hard as she needed to. But her body doesn't hesitate, as she feared it would. She aims for Joanna's belly, and the movement is strong and committed, the point of the blade about to bury itself in the old woman's soft abdomen.

But she realizes right away how badly she miscalculated. Because Joanna may be an old woman, she may be finished with her life of hunting innocent creatures down, but she's still a Knight.

In the space of a breath, Joanna draws a dagger from the sheath over her spine, and counters Ala's blade. At the same time, she elbows Ala hard in the jaw, so hard she sees stars and lurches back, gasping.

Desperate, Ala projects the darkness illusion that she favors, the one that renders her opponent blind. The problem with her illusions is that she has to see them, too; she's never figured out how to exempt herself from the projection. But she knows where Joanna was when she saw her last, so she rushes forward with her arms outstretched and collides with the Knight's legs, shoving her back into the wall.

A line of heat along her arm; Joanna cut her, but not very deep. Or maybe Ala is just choking on adrenaline and can no longer feel pain. She stabs, and the illusion fails just in time for her to see her knife buried in Joanna's leg. The old woman roars and kicks Ala off her, sending her sprawling on the dirt.

Ala is ready with another illusion, this one inspired by her memory of the zmora. She makes herself look like a bear

and then a snake

and then a fox.

She's hoping the reminder of the zmora Joanna once killed will destabilize her. And it seems to—the Knight's steps falter, though she keeps coming, and Ala tries to roll out of the way, but Joanna is too fast. She's already grabbing Ala by the ankle and punching her in the gut by the time Ala registers movement.

As Joanna's fingers close over Ala's throat, she thinks, *It was a mistake to come here.* She thought she knew how fast Knights are, how strong, she thought she *understood*—

But as Dymitr said, there's knowing and there's knowing.

"Tell me, zmora," Joanna asks her, as she chokes Ala. "How many of your kind have you watched die?"

This time, Ala isn't interested in joining in the banter. She's busy imagining the courtyard from Joanna's perspective. The tangle of greenery and the bits of gravel; the side of the house lit blue by the moon. She imagines it without Ala there to interrupt the flow of space. And then, like she's tearing out a piece of fabric, she twists away and stitches herself a few feet to the right, so Joanna will think she's somewhere she isn't.

It's a trap, and Joanna falls into it, swinging at the illusory Ala and ignoring the one right in front of her. Her dagger hits nothing but air.

Ala is already moving toward her when she realizes she made another critical error:

Joanna's last swing was a feint.

Her weight has already shifted, and she's stabbing low and fast at Ala's undefended side. She buries the blade in Ala's gut. Ala screams.

18

A RAZOR'S EDGE

The first time Niko killed a Knight, he was ready to die. Statistically speaking, that was the most likely outcome for a strzygoń who had just taken the zemsta oath. Most of them rushed in too fast and got skewered by a bone sword and then the next strzygoń in the database, some cousin creature, a Greek strix or a Jewish estrie or even the rare Japanese tatarimokke—who could fully shift into owls, something Niko can't even imagine—would be called forward for the job.

So Niko didn't rush in too fast the first time. He got a tip from a double-crosser in Boston that a Knight had come calling about a suspected changeling, and he flew out there a few days after taking his oath. The oath made it so he could do simple tracking spells, so he used them to sniff the Knight out, to plant a few rumors, to lure them to the place of his choosing, and so on.

In the end, though, it came down to sword against sword. And you couldn't really prepare for what it was like to cross blades with a Knight. They were all good at it—every single one Niko had come across. They trained from childhood. And more than that, they were driven by the deep conviction that anyone they drew their sword against was a soulless, life-sucking, humanity-torturing being that *needed to die*. No matter how much Niko hated Knights, he could never believe that of them in return . . . because he simply didn't believe that anyone was beyond redemption.

Which is how he'd ended up in this pickle to begin with.

But his first Knight—

His first Knight was American, not Polish. There were chapters of the Holy Order, after all, in almost every country in the world. And the Knight was a boy, too—only eighteen. Acne dusted his cheeks and he was still gangly with youth and Niko desperately didn't want to kill him. So Niko almost got himself killed, instead. Because when that *child* drew his bone sword, and his eyes turned bloodred, and he came at Niko with all the strength and fervor in his body, it was damn hard to survive him.

But one thing Knights usually weren't was tricky, and Niko was born with a superabundance of trickiness. So some clever footwork and some well-timed light spells—always his favorite—caught the Knight off guard. The boy ended up bleeding out in a little alley next to some trash cans. To be disposed of the following day by the local family of banshees.

One thing Niko never told anyone is that he requested a mass for the Knight. The boy was young, after all, even if he was on a mission to murder a *changeling,* which was really just a child—albeit a child of a very different nature.

The whole debacle was an important lesson in preparation: its importance, and also its insufficiency.

Marzena paces the edge of the weapons room, and Niko listens to her footsteps. Sometimes he learns things from listening that he doesn't learn from watching, though his kind have both good vision and good hearing, as a rule. From Marzena, he learns that she's favoring her right leg. She must have injured herself on her recent hunt.

The weapons room is hexagonal, though the exterior of this part of the house is round. A bench that must have been taken from an old church is leaning against the wall near the door, and all along the walls are cabinets that Niko assumes hold weapons. They're locked, so they're of no use to him, but they're made of dusty, rough wood, like an old ship. And above him, etched into the vaulted wood ceiling, are protective symbols—some of them are Catholic, some not, like a six-pointed rosette, or a triquetra, or an Auseklis cross.

Niko puzzles over them. He knows the Knights' belief system has no real depth to it—every culture has Knights, and Knights always use the religious rhetoric of whatever place they come from to justify killing monsters—but he thought there was at least the *appearance* of consistency. It seems he was wrong.

"Do they trouble you?" Marzena asks him, and she sounds polite, if detached. He's not surprised she hasn't attacked him yet. From what he's heard of Marzena, she loves to play with her food before she eats it.

"I can look at them without bursting into flames, if that's what you mean." Maybe he should attack her right now, before she's ready for it—but there may also be value in learning as much as he can about her before he does.

"When I was young, I believed in them." She wiggles her tattooed fingers at Niko. "But now I'm aware they have no true power. There's nothing otherworldly about you."

"Oh really?" Niko laughs a little. "The fact that I can make you see things that aren't there, that seems completely ordinary to you?"

"A hallucinogenic mushroom can also make me see things that aren't there. I don't call them supernatural, either."

Niko raises his eyebrows. "That's a good point, actually. And here I was thinking all Knights were mindless brutes."

Marzena stops in front of him and folds her arms. She's wiry, her body all sinews and tendons.

"The wieszczy was your doing, wasn't it?" she says. "How did you get it to cooperate? I found it to be . . . rather stubborn, myself."

"Let me tell you the secret to getting any creature to do your bidding," Niko says, and he leans closer, theatrical. "You have to *realize they're people* and *treat them accordingly*."

Marzena smiles.

"Let me tell *you* a secret, zmora," she says. "I have never been under the impression that you and your kind are soulless monsters, or whatever the usual Knight sermons are these days. I believe what my eyes see, which is that you have feelings, you have families, you have all the same shit we have." She rolls her eyes, like families and feelings are just inconveniences—and to her, perhaps they are. She doesn't strike Niko as particularly *maternal,* whatever that really means.

She goes on: "We're all just meat, I know that. Animals, eating whatever food we find, and trying to keep other creatures from killing us. But your kind *feeds* on my kind—you're our only natural predator. You're fast and strong and long-lived, and you have strange abilities we don't fully comprehend. The way I see it, our only advantage is that we outnumber you. And it's my job—my duty, as a member of the human race—to make sure it stays that way." She shrugs. "I take no particular joy in killing a harmless little zmora. It's nothing personal."

"Can't really say the same. For me, it's definitely a little bit personal." Niko smiles. "And I'm not a zmora, you idiot."

And then he lets the ropes that Ala pretended to bind his hands with fall away . . . and he transforms, shrugging off the temporary body Ala loaned him like it's a suit that he's grown out of, and relaxing into his sowa form, the owl version of himself that shifts beneath the surface of him, always waiting to emerge.

It's painful to change—it always is—but it feels like wiggling a loose tooth, the way the beak grows out of his mouth, the way the fine hairs all over his skin turn into feathers, the way his eyeballs elongate, pulled backward into his skull like taffy. Wings grow from the bones of his spine, so rapidly they're just a white-hot burst of agony before they explode from his back, and talons split open his fingertips. All of it happens in a flurry of sensation, and he's already launching himself into the air to collide with Marzena Myśliwiec, the Razor, with all the force he can muster.

He carves ten long, bright gashes into her chest, and she screams—not like she's afraid, but like she's *enraged*. He's not prepared for how ready she is to make use of the pain he gave her. She spits a spell at him, hurling him backward with a powerful breath of wind, and he slams into the cabinets as she puts both hands behind her head and buries her blunt fingernails in her flesh.

He hears it, this time. The splitting of skin and the piercing of muscle, the way her bones creak and crack to release the sword. She breathes hard and fast, and red stains her palms, her arms. Red stains her eyes, too, making her look like—of all things—a vampire from an old movie.

He lands on his feet, his balance aided by his wings. Marzena is already on top of him, swinging her bone sword hard at his head; he just manages to roll away as the blade lands, breaking one of the planks on the cabinet door with its force.

He twists and kicks at her left leg, the one she's so careful to take weight away from when she walks, and she howls, grabbing her knee with her free hand.

He uses her moment of distraction to reach into the cabinet she broke open and grab the first sword he can get his hands on. It's a szabla—a little old, if the roughness of the blade is any indication, and a little curved. Heavy at the hilt, but he adjusts to it, letting the owl sink back into him as he charges his opponent.

He's even-footed and he uses the saber as a cudgel, bashing at Marzena's head. She blocks him and pushes him back with that startling Knight strength. Light on his feet, he rebounds, but only in time to defend himself against three blows in quick succession. The impact makes his wrist ache; Marzena is stronger than the last Knight he fought, though smaller, and he's not sure how that's possible, unless it's by magic—

He tries to cut her, but she only laughs, and digs her bloody fingers into one of the gashes he left her at the start of all this.

"Rozszczep," she says, in a tone of command, and the skin over his heart simply . . . splits open, like a burst grape. Blood runs hot down Niko's torso, and he swallows a scream, but she hasn't finished.

"Złam!" she commands, pressing down again with her

fingers in her own wound, and one of his fingers twists in the wrong direction and cracks, the bone unmistakably breaking—

—and in her smile, he sees that no amount of preparation could have aided him in this task. She's fearless and she's ready and she has a mouth full of Knight curses and he gave her all the pain she would need to use them.

He really was sent here to die.

19

A WHIFF OF PERFUME

Dymitr is familiar with pain. *Pain is a part of any life,* his grandmother used to say. *But for a Knight it's even more essential.* Pain was where their magic came from, it was the sacrifice that magic required, but it needed no bargaining, no deal-making, no pleading, as other forms of magic did. Pain magic was control, it was command. *Pain is power.*

This pain is not like that.

This pain is completely out of his control. He feels like a piece of pottery with crazing on its surface; every tiny crack is white-hot agony, and they're spreading across his skin in a web. He no longer feels right leg, left leg, right arm, left arm—all he feels is the hurt, and all he wants is an escape from it. He wants that escape so badly he would gladly invite any other kind of pain, a blow to the head or a hammer to his hand, if it meant feeling *something else* for a while.

He's so far gone he can't figure out who's who. He can't figure out if it's Ala he's in the courtyard with, Ala wearing the illusion of his face, or if it's Niko, transformed into his likeness by magic. He forces himself to breathe in through his nose, even though all he wants to do is pant like a dog; he tries to focus long enough to smell something, anything.

He smells—airplane, and wet earth, and the candy-apple soap from the hotel, and the flavorless sweet of powdered sugar.

Ala.

He wants to sob. Ala is trapped in a courtyard with his grandmother.

The two of them are talking, and then the illusion drops and she's there as herself, the same height as Joanna but nowhere near as strong. Zmoras are built for escaping, for deceiving—not for this, blade against blade, strength against strength, in the confined space of the courtyard. Ala is capable, but she's not trained, and she's not a Knight.

Through the haze of pain, he looks down at Ala's feet. She's wearing the socks he mended.

He thinks of her standing in front of the pot of ramen, asking him what he smells. He thinks of her kneeling on the floor in Baba Jaga's apartment, begging him to *try*.

Ala saved his soul. But his grandmother only ever split it in half.

He forces himself to move. One foot and then another, digging into the earth for a foothold. He wraps his hands around stinging nettles and pulls himself to his hands and knees. His grandmother and Ala are swinging at each other, and then—

And then his grandmother stabs Ala low in her abdomen, right next to her hip. Ala's scream rattles in his head, and he's on his feet—just barely, but he's upright. Both Ala and his grandmother are facing away from him, like they've forgotten he's even there.

He has no weapons. His hands twitch, the instinct to draw the bone sword that's no longer buried in his body aborted at the last second. When he raises his head to look at the statue of Saint Michael, though, he remembers the little knife fixed to the statue's back, only a little sturdier than a letter opener.

He limps toward it, each step reawakening new pain, and grabs the handle of the small knife with his trembling hand. His grandmother has her hand around Ala's throat, forcing her to her knees with a gurgle. Dymitr's vision goes dark at the edges.

He lets the Knight in him surface—he has plenty of pain to feed the transformation, even if he doesn't have his sword to urge it along. Red creeps over his palms and heat surges into his eyes.

He can see the shadow in Ala, the restless thing, and he thinks, *Maybe it's her soul I'm seeing, maybe that's all we could ever see—*

The transformation gives him strength, even if it doesn't take away the pain. He crosses the courtyard in two big strides.

He slides the knife between his grandmother's ribs.

She gasps—wheezes—but she's already moving, even

as she's reacting to the pain. She whirls around to face him, stabbing down with her knife.

He brings his left arm up to block her. Her mouth falls open a little as she looks into his eyes.

His eyes, which are red to match hers.

"Dymek?" she says weakly.

"Babcia," he replies.

Her blood runs hot over his fingers. Ala is face down in the dirt behind her, bleeding and stinking of terror.

"What has . . ." His grandmother gasps. "Become of you?"

He has no words to explain it, and she wouldn't understand it if he did. He's a zmora; he's a Knight. He's the same Dymitr he always was; he's brand new. *Magic is crooked,* Baba Jaga said, and he can see it more clearly now than ever before, how magic embraces paradox. But his grandmother's mind doesn't work that way.

Blood bubbles up over her lips as she says, "Monster."

She yanks her hand back and stabs again, and after all this—after the accusations and the torture and the curses, after all the evidence of what she is laid out before him—he's still surprised by it. He's still surprised by the fervor in her eyes and her gritted teeth and the powerful swing of her arm.

But before she can cut into him, she falls. She drops to her knees, one leg stretched out behind her. Ala's pale hand is wrapped around her ankle.

Dymitr catches his grandmother by instinct, just to

ease her to the ground. The red in her eyes and hands recedes. Her breaths rattle and wheeze. The scent of mustard and dirt and peach nectar and candy-apple soap fills his nose.

Followed by the faintest hint of his grandmother's floral perfume.

A PARTING SHOT

Niko is pretty sure he's about to die, but he's not one to give up in the middle of a fight. He swings the saber at Marzena's head, and she bats him aside harder than is necessary, which wrenches his broken finger. Her smile sharpens by a fraction and then she comes at him.

Whatever she was doing before was just a warm-up. This is the real thing: Marzena hacking at him with all the force of her muscled, magically strengthened body. It's all he can do to counter each blow, his shoulder aching with the effort of holding the saber aloft.

He should transform again, but it would take a split second he *doesn't have,* because she's putting so much pressure on him he can hardly breathe. She's herding him back toward the wall, so he'll have no room to evade her; he knows that, but he also can't stop it.

He listens to the shuffle of their feet, the clang of their swords colliding, the heaving of his own breaths. But all he can see is her, eyes bright, jaw clenched, body in constant motion.

He feels the wood against his back, and brings the saber up at an awkward angle to catch her blade close to his abdomen. She slides bone against metal all the way down to the hilt of his sword, and grins crookedly at him.

"How would you like to die?" she asks him, roughly. "Bleeding, or suffocation?"

He wishes he had some kind of clever answer. She whispers the spell to break his bones again, and he hears something deep inside him cracking, and a sharp agony in his rib cage. Suddenly it's even harder to breathe than before; he sees spots as she presses him down even harder, trying to force him to his knees.

"Złam," she spits, and another one of his ribs *pops*. He screams into gritted teeth.

The wood against his back reminds him of the warm metal of the fence earlier that day, Dymitr's hands in his shirt, the prickling of his frustration over Niko's skin. It's not a bad memory to go out with, really. Dymitr is beautiful like a Rembrandt painting, the only focal point in a room of darkness, expressive and *significant* somehow. And he can see Dymitr in Marzena's face, just a hint of him, so if he tries, he can pretend—

He goes to his knees, but he keeps pressing up against Marzena's sword. Then he sees, as if for the first time, her boots. Knee-high. Leather. Scuffed everywhere, like she's never bothered to polish them, with the laces all frayed. The same aura of carelessness that Dymitr carries around;

he must have learned it from her. Her weight is off her left foot; it's the one she injured—and there's something else about it, something at the very edge of his thoughts—

She keeps a knife in her left boot, Dymitr said to him, right before they parted ways. Niko sees the knife handle poking out of the top of it. He's reaching for it before he even decides to. He yanks it free and then stabs up, not at her belly but at her arm.

The knife goes between the bones of her forearm, slicing through tendons and arteries and muscle. Marzena's grip on her bone sword falters, and he wrenches away from her, still on his knees. Her sword clatters to the ground, and he twists, kicking her in the left knee.

She sprawls, falling to the stone, and he grabs her bone sword in his left hand, leaving her with the knife stuck through her arm. He's on his feet in an instant, holding the blade she made from half her soul right up against her throat.

She looks up at him. Her forehead is sweaty and her breathing is labored.

Her eyes are gray.

"Do it," she spits at him.

Niko curses himself. He curses the wieszczy who agreed to help him and Ala with her nerves of steel, and Dymitr with his fucking gray eyes. But mostly . . . he curses himself, for letting himself be softened by all those things.

"You're lucky your son is so beautiful," he says.

And because he's not a saint, he kicks her in the side

before limping out of the room, her bone sword still in his hand.

�֍

When Niko steps out of the weapons room, Ala and Dymitr are in the hallway, bloody and pale as death. Dymitr's gaze fixes over Niko's shoulder at the still-writhing—still *living*—form of his mother on the floor behind him. He doesn't seem to understand what he's looking at; Ala has to snap her fingers in front of his face to remind him they need to get moving.

And when Niko moves to put the bone sword down on a side table, Dymitr's eyes bear down on his with startling intensity.

"Take it," he says roughly.

So Niko does.

They go out the back and into the woods, though the woods aren't much of a comfort out here, not when Knights are well trained in tracking. At a certain point, when they're far enough from the house that the pressure of the Knights' magic eases a little and Ala says she can no longer smell copper, they stop so that Niko can heal the worst of their injuries: the wound in Ala's hip, Niko's broken bones, and some of the deeper gashes on Dymitr's back.

Niko's hands shake when he lays them on Dymitr's bloody shoulders, and he tries not to think about what it must have felt like for his own mother to cut into him like that, over and over again, with the pain magnified by ten.

When Niko asks about that particular curse, though, Dymitr just shakes his head. "Gone now," he says, and he doesn't elaborate. Niko puts the pieces together himself: the curse ended when Joanna's life did.

Walking through the hotel where Ala and Dymitr are staying, all of them soaked in blood, is one of the most absurd things Niko has done lately, but he addles the night manager's senses enough that he's pretty sure she'll dismiss it as a dream the following morning. Ala meets Niko's eyes once they're in the room, and nods toward the bathroom.

Niko leads Dymitr in with him and closes the door.

They've had a little Florence Nightingale moment before, in the hospice center, with Dymitr's lost fingernail. Niko thinks about it all the time, the way something was crackling between them, but Niko wasn't sure if he was reading it right; the way Dymitr's eyes went wide when Niko called him beautiful; the ache Niko felt in his chest when they first kissed.

Well, this isn't like that.

There's nothing sexy-sweet about peeling the blood-soaked shirt from Dymitr's body, or listening to his harsh breaths, or surveying the damage his own mother did to him. All Niko can do is try not to stare. He crouches in front of Dymitr and takes off his boots for him.

"You didn't kill her," Dymitr says roughly. "Why?"

And Niko says, "You know why."

He straightens. Dymitr reaches for Niko's hand. His

hold a little too tight, he brings their clasped hands to his chest. Niko feels the hard thump of Dymitr's heart.

"Dziękuję," Dymitr says, and it's as solemn as a vow. *Thank you.*

As Dymitr strips down and steps into the shower, Niko splashes water on his face at the sink, and takes off his shirt to examine the magical wound Marzena gave him just by commanding his skin to split. It's not pretty, and it's still bleeding. He should probably stitch it; maybe there's a sewing kit in one of the drawers.

Then he hears Dymitr sobbing like he's trying to keep it quiet, and he thinks, *Fuck it,* and he gets into the shower, too, still half-clothed and determined to ignore the sudden intimacy of Dymitr's nakedness as he gathers the other man close.

The water is so warm it's almost too hot, and the hotel soap smells like a Jolly Rancher. Dymitr tucks his face into the side of Niko's neck. He holds Niko so tightly they meld together, Dymitr's shaking body against his, the water drumming against Niko's back. He runs his fingers through Dymitr's wet hair, and doesn't say anything, because there's nothing to say.

A MEETING OF SISTERS

Elza is the best tracker, so while the others deal with the aftermath—with her grandmother's body, rendered small and frail in death; with the knife speared through her mother's arm; with the wieszczy who appeared at Filip's grave and then vanished, seemingly without a trace; with the grave itself, waiting for Filip's body to fill it; with her young cousin André, who disappeared sometime in the night; with all of it, the whole fucking nightmare of it all—

While the others deal with the aftermath, Elza follows the trail into town.

In truth, there's no need for the best tracker to complete this task. The three intruders who turned everything in her life upside down last night didn't go to much effort to disguise their tracks. They left bloody, muddy footprints through the forest, then stopped—to heal themselves, she thinks, because the footprints became less bloody after that—and then continued into town, where they walked right into a hotel. All Elza had to do to figure out what room they were in was wait for a light to go on.

The intruders, that's how she thinks of them now.

Because that man, the one who killed her grandmother, can't possibly be Dymitr. He has to be some *thing* wearing Dymitr's face again, or Dymitr himself has to be cursed, his mind addled by magic—because the alternative is impossible.

Isn't it?

She creeps up to a window, and draws her bone swords, her teeth gritted with fury as she remembers the way her grandmother's face looked, so pale, her eyes still open but unseeing. She's here to exact bloody vengeance on all three of them, and she's going to start by climbing through the bathroom window to ambush them while they're still hurt and exhausted from their escape. She's going to start *right now.*

She reaches up to see if the window is unlocked, and hears . . . sobbing.

She braces herself against the stucco wall. She knows that sound. She's heard it just a few times before, through the paper-thin walls of their house, through the bathroom door, but it's not easy to forget the sound of your older brother falling apart.

That's him.

That's really him.

She goes still, her body gripped with fear as she realizes the Dymitr she spent dinner trading knowing looks with was not, in fact, some zmora skilled with illusions and mimicry, or some strzygoń wearing a magical skin, but the real him.

And somehow, the real him . . . is now a monster.

Baba Jaga must have cursed him. That's the only explanation she can think of. Baba Jaga cursed him, and he was too afraid to tell anyone what happened because he thought they would kill him, and—and he was right to fear that, because her mother would have spent the night torturing him for information and then, whether he gave it or not, slit his throat at sunrise.

But that doesn't explain why he lied to protect the zmora. Or why there's a murmur just audible through the glass— the strzygoń, its voice deep and rumbling as an engine, trying to soothe him.

She doesn't understand. She doesn't understand, and she needs to, or this bloody night will haunt her for the rest of her life. So she sheathes her swords and decides to wait.

It takes hours for anything to happen. Elza knows she should go home, if she's not going to act—go home, and change into her funeral clothes, so she can be there when they bury Filip. But she can't make herself move. Not until she understands what happened to her brother.

Around sunrise, the zmora steps out of the hotel and walks down the road. Elza follows it all the way to the forest again.

The light is weak and pale, and there's dew clinging to all the spiderwebs. When Elza finds herself getting too close to the zmora, she stops to examine one, a symmetrical orb weaver's web with the spider herself perched in the middle, her legs curled up around her.

The zmora isn't making much effort to move quietly. It ducks under branches and hops over logs and swats at the little flies that are already out in force. It keeps pausing to sniff the air, like a hunting dog. Whatever scent it's following, it follows all the way to the fort where Elza, Kazik, and Dymitr used to play as children.

Elza grits her teeth. *No,* she thinks. *It can't be.*

The zmora can't possibly know.

The fort is in a small clearing. The structure itself is built between two tall trees at the edge of the space, and it's made of thin branches lined up next to each other like slats. Elza and Kazik spent days searching the forest floor for the right ones, then they brought them to Dymitr, who was the only one patient enough to saw off the ends to make them all even. The top of the fort is neat and tidy, as a result.

The zmora slips through the opening to the fort, and Elza thinks about killing it right here. It would be simple enough to draw her bone swords again and corner the zmora in the fort; it would happen too quickly for the monster to devise some clever illusion to get away. But then she wouldn't be any closer to answers.

Through the fort's uneven branches, Elza can see the zmora kneeling beside the metal lunch pail that's nestled in the corner of the structure. Elza is the one who put it there, the one who nestled the book of curses inside it to keep it safe.

The zmora *does* know.

It lifts its head, and through the gap between the branches, Elza meets its eyes.

"How did you know the book was here?" Elza says.

The zmora draws a knife. Elza can see the metal glinting through the branches.

"I'm not here to kill you," Elza says. "Not today, anyway."

She holds her hands out in front of her, so the zmora can see that she's not armed. She could become armed in a matter of seconds, of course, but she's not eager to draw her swords right now. The zmora goes to the door of the fort, a knife in one hand and the blue book of curses in the other.

"I saw this place last night," the zmora says. "Thought I'd take a look."

Last night. It sounds so casual to Elza, like last night wasn't a series of horrors. But then, as a creature who's named after the nightmare itself, maybe it doesn't think of betrayal and deception and murder as a series of horrors.

Last night—the empty night.

Remember the last things, the singers sang. *The clock is ticking, death is cutting down the tree of life.*

"What are you here for, if not to kill me?" the zmora asks Elza, and Elza can't think of the last time she spoke to a monster like this. It has such a human face. High cheekbones, sharp, almost wild eyes. It could be someone Elza went to school with, someone Elza passed on the street. Ordinary. Pretty, even.

"Answers," Elza says. "If I get them, I won't kill you. Provided you leave that book behind."

"We'll see" is the zmora's response.

"Last night." Grief rises up in Elza's throat like vomit. She swallows it down. "That was really him?"

The zmora doesn't respond, at first. It sniffs the air, looking thoughtful.

"Do you know," it says, "a zmora can tell the difference between dread and fear. A person fears what's unknown, but they dread what's known. What you're feeling right now smells very much like dread. So I can tell that you already know the answer to your own question."

"A yes would have sufficed."

"I'm not sure it would have, actually. Because if you're going to have a zmora for a brother, you should really understand more about our kind than 'monster bad, monster needs to die.'"

"I do not have a . . . a *monster* for a brother. If that thing is what my brother is now, then my brother is dead."

"Your brother, who is not a 'thing,' killed the person he loves most to save my life yesterday," the zmora replies. "So you'll talk about him with respect, or you can fuck right off."

Elza only notices that her cheeks are wet with tears when a breeze blows cool against her skin. She wipes them with the heel of her hand.

"Who cursed him with this?" Elza asks. "And how? Can it be undone?"

"It probably can. But since he's the one who asked for it to begin with, I'm pretty sure it won't be."

"Don't lie to me. He would never *ask* for this."

The zmora tilts her head. "Are you sure about that? Are we talking about the brother who doesn't like when you call us 'monsters'?"

Elza opens her mouth to argue further, but she can't help remembering. Dymitr, sobbing after his first kill instead of celebrating. Dymitr, calling the strzyga who killed their uncle "she" instead of "it." Dymitr, sparring with Elza in the street to keep her from killing the strzygoń.

If she thinks back to everything he said to her in Chicago, and everything she said to him, it makes a certain amount of sense. He chose his words so carefully. She asked him if Baba Jaga was his target; he said he wouldn't discuss it with her. She told him he was acting strange; he said, *I am doing what's necessary.*

What's necessary.

"Why?" Her voice breaks over the word. "Why would he ever want this?"

"Because he wanted to stop being a murderer," the zmora says. "Which is really all a Knight is, once you strip away the rhetoric."

Elza's face burns hot as a fever. "We're fighting for humanity—"

The zmora holds up the book of curses. "If you really believe that, why did you hide this here?"

Elza went looking for a secret message from Dymitr right after he left for America. She assumed he would leave one in the bathroom cabinet, explaining why he was going on this mission alone. Instead, she found the book of curses. She remembers kneeling on the bath mat and flipping through it, her skin crawling. She knows the methods for killing most things—what needs a blade through the heart, what needs its head chopped off, what needs to be burned or salted or buried at a full moon. But the torments written on those pages made her feel sick.

So she brought the book here. She still doesn't understand why, not fully.

"The book scared me," Elza says. "I didn't want anyone else to find it."

"It scared you because it's a handbook for creative torture," the zmora says. "And deep down, you know that it's horrible to do those things to a living creature. You know that you don't like what it says about your people, that they've done those things so many times they decided to write them down. And now, hopefully, you know that if this book falls into the wrong hands, those horrors can be inflicted on your brother."

The zmora steps closer, but only a little.

"And he *is* still your brother, Elza," the zmora says. "He's kind, and quiet, and he'll mend your socks without being asked, and he leaves orange peels everywhere, and he's got incredible aim. He's Dymitr."

Elza is crying again. She tells herself it's because she's mourning the loss of him. That the creature that now wears his face is just an echo of him. It can do the things he used to do, but it's no longer him, it no longer has his soul or his heart or his mind.

The zmora says, "Let me take the book so no one can use it against him. Please."

A tear rolls off the end of Elza's chin. She looks away, into the brightening woods. "If I cross paths with you again, I won't be merciful."

The zmora smiles a little too wide—like the Cheshire cat from the old cartoon, just teeth aglow in the dark woods.

"Neither will I," it says.

AN AIRPLANE MOVIE

Niko pays for their tickets home. They sit together on the plane, all three of them in a row, with Dymitr in the middle seat. Ala waits until after the meal has come and gone and Niko has fallen asleep against the window to take the book of curses out of her bag. She sets it on Dymitr's tray table like it's an old magazine.

He stares down at it, gray eyes wide.

He's bruised. On his jaw, around his eye, on his cheek. His lip is split, too. She hates to look at those wounds, knowing he endured all of that because he refused to give her up to his grandmother and his mother. When she thinks about that, she gets an uncomfortable feeling in her throat like she swallowed a grapefruit whole.

"How did you . . ." He looks up at her. "*Where—*"

"You were very insistent that only you and Elza knew about the bathroom hiding place, so when the book wasn't there, I figured she had found it and moved it," Ala says. "And last night, when we were dragging our broken selves through the woods, I saw the fort and I felt . . ." She taps her temple. "That Knight magic thing."

"Brilliant," he says breathlessly.

"Your sister found me there."

That startles him. His head jerks up.

"She knew it was really you, last night," Ala says. "I asked her to let me keep the book so it couldn't be used to hurt you."

"And?" he asks, his voice soft.

"And she let me go. I think . . . there's hope for her. Just a little sliver of it, but . . . some."

Dymitr's eyes are bright. He takes the book and slides it into his backpack. He's zipping it back up and pushing it under the seat in front of him when Ala finally works up the courage to say, "There's some things I need to say to you before I lose my voice to that wiła for a few days. The first is that I misled you. I told you I came here to help you, and that was mostly a lie—I came here to kill her. Joanna."

Dymitr doesn't react. Doesn't move at all, in fact—just stares at her, waiting.

"I've been having nightmares that replay everything the curse showed me. Especially about her. I thought if she was dead, I would get some peace. And I thought, because I'd seen so many memories of Knights, I knew how to fight them." She closes her eyes. Swallows hard. "But none of that was true."

She dreamed about Joanna last night, in fact. The same memory, playing again. She woke with the same trembling in her hands, and realized she'd been thinking of the aftermath of the curse as a puzzle to be solved. If she could just get the letters in the right place, she would be free from it. But there's no puzzle. Only a tangle. A knot that will take a lifetime to untie.

"The second thing I want to say is," she says, "I—I'm sorry. I know how much you loved your grandmother, and that you only had to do that to her because I couldn't manage to do it myself. And now I'll always be the one you did that for, and . . . I'm sorry."

Dymitr seizes her hand. His grip is warm and strong.

"Never . . . *never* say that to me again," he says, quiet but insistent.

Ala wipes her tears away with her fingers.

"What you will always be to me now," he says, "is my sister, who I love and want to be safe. Understand?"

Their hands are clasped over the narrow metal armrest.

Ala nods. A garbled voice speaks over the intercom, warning them about upcoming turbulence. A man in a hooded sweatshirt squeezes past Ala's seat in the aisle. The intensity between them passes, though Ala still feels unsteady, like she's about to scream or sob or laugh out loud.

"Want a chip?" Dymitr says, and it should be strange that he's still holding her hand, but it isn't. It feels nice, instead.

"Are you referring to the hardened, salted paste of your preferred airport snack?" she says. "Because I don't really think they qualify as 'chips.'"

He grins at her—as much as he can, anyway, without reopening the split in his lip.

She leans her head on his shoulder, and he turns on a movie, and she thinks that if she's going to spend her life untangling all this pain, at least she has someone she cares about to do it with.

At least she has him.

A BONE SWORD

Baba Jaga likes to go for walks on summer nights in Chicago. Even she isn't immune to the charms of this time of year. She wraps herself in a younger woman's skin and walks the hot sidewalks with people coming in from the beach, still covered in sand. She lets panting dogs trot alongside her and nudge her with their wet noses. She listens to the screeching of the cicadas and the lapping of Lake Michigan against the rocks that hold it at bay. She swats at mosquitos and spots robins plucking fireflies out of the air and teenagers hiding their beers when they hear her approach.

The Knight is sitting on her steps when she returns to her house that evening. His face is spotted black-and-blue, and he sits like that's not the worst of it, but it's his aura that concerns her most. He wears his sorrow like a very heavy crown, indeed. The banshees and lloronas of the neighborhood could all feast on him at once and still leave sated.

He looks up at her, and *sniffs*—such a zmora greeting, they're like a pack of dogs that way, only trusting their noses. He seems to recognize who she really is, but he doesn't move out of her way, or come to his feet to let her pass. He's here to be an obstruction.

She sighs. "You've piqued my curiosity, Knight. You can come in."

He stands up, then. Stiff as an old man in his movements, and she wonders if she should offer to heal him just so she doesn't have to see him wince like that. But not until she knows where the pain came from—not until she knows what it's teaching him.

She climbs the creaky steps with their worn carpet, the smell of fried chicken following her all the way to the third-floor landing. The door opens for her, and the apartment lights up at her approach, every lamp at once. The lava lamp in the corner over the table of bones; the pink art deco lamp with the fringe shade; the lamp with the Tiffany-style shade covered in blue flowers; the fairy lights strung over one of the archways that wink on and off every second. She unwraps the shawl that makes her look like a younger, lighter-haired woman, and hangs it on a hook on the wall.

Beneath it, she's old and weathered, which suits her mood. There's gray mixed with the black of her long, thick hair. She beckons for the Knight to follow her deeper into the apartment, and stands before the apothecary table where she once mixed the cure for what ailed him.

Now, she arranges the ingredients for a healing potion, just in case she decides to give it to him. A thin slice of dried starfish, a tiny spoonful of salamander eyes, a pinch of yarrow root, three drops of aloe vera, a preserved calendula petal. She puts them in the huge mortar, but doesn't crush them with the pestle yet.

"And so?" she says to the Knight.

"I've come to make a deal with you," he replies.

She laughs, and takes up the pestle. It's so big it only just fits in her hand; hardly necessary for this particular blend, but she grinds the eyes and the petal and the yarrow and the starfish slice into a paste with the aloe vera.

"You came here before as a supplicant, and now you're here as a businessman," she says. "What changed?"

He hesitates, and she hears a murmur in that hesitation that interests her. She cocks her head, and then looks over her shoulder at his bruised face.

"You killed her," she says softly.

His expression is answer enough, but when he opens his mouth to speak he seems unable to produce any sound at all. He closes his mouth.

She sets the pestle down and presses her palm to the paste she's made of all the healing ingredients. She drags her fingers around the edge of the mortar to smear the sticky substance over her fingers. It's yellow-brown and grainy.

"Hold still," she says to the Knight, and she touches her thumb to the bruise on his cheek. He pulls away.

"I'm going to heal you, child," she says. "It's disconcerting to see you this way."

She dabs his cheek with her thumb, and uses her index finger for the delicate skin around his eye, her pinkie finger for the cut on his lip, her middle finger for the stained skin on his forehead. The paste shines for just a moment before sinking into him, and it takes each wound with it.

By the time she's finished, he looks just as he did a week ago, when he pleaded for his sword. She wipes her hand on the handkerchief she retrieves from her pocket, and then tosses it behind her. It disappears into thin air.

"Better," she says, and then she gestures—a request— and the house, ever-generous, provides. Two chairs appear in front of her, facing each other. She takes one, and she glares at the Knight until he takes the other, sitting on the very edge of it.

"Do you know that a complete transformation is almost impossible?" she asks. "Something of the old version usually remains. My grandson, for example, will probably never live as long or age as slowly as most of his kind. I warned him of this before I made him what he is. It didn't seem to trouble him, but then, he did always have a thread of cheerful nihilism in him."

She smiles at the memory of little Nikodem Kostka, dragged into her apartment by his terrified mother who couldn't stomach the eventuality of death. She shooed the woman for the actual transformation, and sat with Niko on the floor, old bones be damned, to tell him it would hurt to become a strzygoń. Niko only shrugged. Already understanding, perhaps, that pain was as meaningless as its lack, and as inevitable.

"I have known of only a few occasions on which a change was comprehensive and unalterable," she says. "One of those occasions, I lived through. I was born human, you see, with no particular aptitude for magic. I made great sacrifices to acquire that aptitude, which I will not enumerate for you now. But in order to make it permanent, I had to endure the unthinkable."

She looks into the Knight's stormy eyes.

"I had to kill the one I loved most in all the world," she says. "It was for the good of all, but that isn't the reason I did it. I did it because I was desperate to change, fully and completely, and I was willing to do anything to accomplish it. Even rip out my own heart."

She says it without emotion. Long ago, she locked her memories of that day in a box and buried them—literally, with a shovel and a lantern in the dead of night, at a place no one else knows. So she can't see the man's face at the moment he realized she betrayed him; she can't remember how it sounded when he breathed his last. It's better that way.

Even though the Knight has every reason to despise her for what she told him to do, he looks a little sad at her recollection. What a soft heart he has, she thinks, and it's as great an impossibility as she has ever seen, for a boy raised as a Knight to have a soft heart.

"Your grandmother had to give her blood to you so that you could split your soul, did she not?" she asks.

The Knight raises his eyebrows. "How did you know that?"

"Your sword sang a little song," Baba Jaga replies. "And I heard it."

The Knight looks down at his hands. "The curse she put me under, when I was there. It ended when she died."

"Another curse born of her blood." Baba Jaga nods.

"So the magic that split my soul." He scratches at the back of his neck, like he's remembering drawing the sword from his spine. "I couldn't be rid of it until she died. That's why you told me to kill her."

She reaches out and touches his knee. "I am often cruel. But I am not usually cruel without reason. This was the crucial first step in making your transformation real and lasting."

His head bobs. Baba Jaga takes her hand away.

"You came here to make me an offer. I think it's time you make it."

The Knight straightens in his chair. "I have in my possession a book of Knights' magic. It's one of the only ones in existence. If you return my sword to me, I'll give it to you."

Baba Jaga smiles. She stands, and walks over to the little bookcase in the corner. The books arranged on it are old and leather-bound, their spines cracked and their pages worn and musty. Sometimes she takes one out just to stick her nose between the pages and breathe in the scent of it.

She takes a slim green volume from the shelf, and offers it to him.

He opens it, and his face falls. It's written in Cyrillic, so he likely can't read the letters, but he seems to recognize the diagram of the bone sword on the first page.

"You mean a book like this?" she says. "I have several. Each one is in a different language. They have significant overlap, but there's always one spell or another that's distinct in each one. I collect them."

The Knight sags in his chair, staring at the drawing of the bone sword. Baba Jaga curls her fingers over the back of her own chair, her dark fingernails drumming against the wood.

"So you see, you still come to me with almost nothing. But all is not lost."

She snaps her fingers—a request—and the cloth-wrapped bone sword floats toward her from its place on the wall, landing gently in her hands. The Knight looks at it like it's a flagon of water and he's dying of thirst.

"I asked you for thirty-three deaths. I will settle for the death of your grandmother in addition to thirty-two broken curses, instead." She starts to unwrap the bone sword, unwinding the black cloth that covers the hilt. "Use that book you stole. Undo some of the harm your people have done. Unravel their magic, and you will earn your full transformation."

A promise sometimes has the feeling of magic. This one certainly does. She lets the black cloth fall, holding the white sword in her hands.

"Do we have a deal?"

"Thirty-two broken curses, and you'll give me back the sword?"

"Thirty-two broken curses, and your soul will be fully healed."

"Zgadzam się," he says. *Agreed*.

"Shirt off, then. And kneel."

He gives her a confused look. But it seems he's beyond defiance. He unbuttons his shirt, and shrugs it from his shoulders. Then he stands from his chair, and kneels in front of her, as he did before she changed him the first time.

Baba Jaga walks around him, bone sword in hand. His back is covered in deep wounds—harsh red lines from the drag of a blade. It's as if he was beaten, only the wounds are too intentional for that. Each one of these was cut into him by a deliberate hand.

She turns the sword so that it's upright, then holds it over his back, so the hilt will stretch across his shoulders, and the blade will follow his spine.

"Ready?" she says.

The Knight nods, and she presses the sword to his back. For a moment it hovers in place right over his skin. Then it shimmers, like the bone is turning to glass. The bright light pricks at her eyes, making them water.

But the bone doesn't turn to glass—it turns to gold. Then the bright wounds on the Knight's back start to pull open like hungry mouths, seeking, undulating with hunger. The Knight screams a horrible scream, but Baba Jaga hardly notices it; she's too busy trying to peer through the glare of the magic to see what will happen next.

The sword presses to the wounds, as if to cauterize them. It sizzles against his skin, and he screams again, falling forward onto his hands. The metal sword sinks into him, but only barely; it stays at the surface of his skin, the perfect impression of a longsword now flush with his back.

The light of the magic fades. The Knight's back shifts with his breaths, the sword flexible enough to accommodate him.

He straightens, and reaches over his shoulder to touch the sword. He looks up at her, eyes full of wonder.

"It's still there?" he says. "But—"

"I told you that complete transformations are nearly impossible," she says. "When you're finished with this task I've given you, you'll have done the impossible, and the sword will be gone. Curse by curse, it will disappear."

He no longer looks sick, she thinks. His cheeks are bright, his eyes lively. She feels . . . better.

"Thank you," he says.

She shrugs, and as she shrugs, her skin tightens, and her gray hair turns dark brown, and buoyancy returns to her joints.

"I want to ask you a favor," she says. "You can count it among your broken curses."

"What is it?" he asks.

She walks away, but pauses before stepping into the next room—the one that's in Hyde Park.

"Protect my grandson," she says. "The Kostkas are trying to get him killed, and I've grown rather fond of him."

A soft reply: "I would have done that anyway."

"I am an excellent negotiator," she says. "So you can assume that when I'm not, it's intentional. Show yourself out."

A LAST DEMAND

The zmora Dryjas have the Crow Theater, and the str-zyga Kostkas have the boxing club, but on the south side of the city where the streets have numbers instead of names, there's a cluster of warehouses and a big, empty house that the llorona Vasquez family has transformed into . . . a nightclub.

"I don't understand," Ala says, as she eases her cousin's beat-up station wagon into a parking spot nearby. "What does a nightclub have to do with sorrow?"

Ala got her voice back from the wiła that morning, and they borrowed the station wagon that afternoon to look for a new apartment. The loss of Ala's voice turned out to be good for both of them—Ala could ask him in writing if he wanted to be her roommate indefinitely, which meant she didn't have to say it out loud, and Dymitr could pick her up and swing her around without her pretending to be upset about it.

They found a crappy two-bedroom basement unit in Irving Park that suited them both, and Ala signed the lease, since Dymitr—or *Dawid Myśliwiec,* as Ala insisted on calling him—is technically still on a temporary visa forged by the Holy Order. Niko said he knew a guy who could get him some convincing fake paperwork, though, so there's that.

Dymitr waits for Ala to straighten out the station wagon in the space—it turns out she's a bit of a parking perfectionist—and then unbuckles his seat belt and gets out.

"The peculiar wisdom of Keeners," he says, using the slang term that refers generally to llorona and banshees and all other sorrow-eating beings from around the world, "is that sorrow is so plentiful, they don't need to hunt for it at all."

"I don't know how *you're* explaining this to *me*," she grumbles. "Mister 'I became a creature of legend ten minutes ago.'"

He slides his hands into his pockets and walks next to her on the sidewalk. He doesn't need to ask where they're going: their destination is obvious.

The house stands between an empty, fenced-off lot and a foreclosed building with a collapsed porch. The building itself is gray, with a gabled roof and blacked-out windows, the kind of place Dymitr would have avoided if he hadn't already known what it was. A group of greenish rusałkas stand outside, passing around a single cigarette, each of them with hair down to their waists. They're dressed for a good time, in skin-baring tops with glittery eye makeup.

The house is a split-level, and upon entering, Dymitr lets

Ala lead them down to the basement instead of upstairs. It's dark inside, and *hot,* from the crowd of bodies that greets them. Purple and blue lights hang in strips along the walls and above them. The ceiling is high—Dymitr thinks they hollowed out the first floor to make the place taller—and there are glow-in-the-dark stars stuck to it.

"My highest priority is beer," Ala announces. "If I'm going to dance, I need to be a little drunk. Do you dance?"

Dymitr shakes his head. He's already scanning the crowd for Niko.

"Oh my God, just go find him already," she says. "Text me when you're done with whatever errand you guys are running."

Dymitr waves goodbye, and steps into the crowd.

He had a feeling this would happen—that every sorrow-eating thing in the vicinity would turn to look at him, their wide eyes shining in the darkness. He knows what he must look like to them, every part of him still aching with grief. They brush him as he passes through the crowd, their fingers on his arms, his shoulders. He shies away from their touches, still looking for Niko.

There's a stage at the back of the room where people are setting up music equipment. A DJ rig, microphones. Someone else is hoisting a disco ball high above the crowd, as if they need more dizzying light than what they already have.

He's just spotted Niko leaning up against a pillar, red cup in hand, when the stage lights turn on and everyone starts clapping and cheering. There's no fear in the air, nothing he can sink his teeth into, but there's an energy all the same.

All the lights go off at once, and then a wordless note pierces the darkness, quiet at first and then louder, higher, filling the entire room with sound. He feels it settling deep inside him, cold and heavy as water. A Keener sound, a banshee wail. Tears prickle behind his eyes as the note claws into him, forcing emotion he doesn't want to feel. Instinctively, he searches for the door, for a path to escape, but he doesn't flee.

The stage lights go on again, and someone standing at the DJ rig taps something in front of him. A beat plays beneath the Keener note, breaking it up into fragments. The woman stops singing and picks up an electric violin, wrapped in glowing tape that lights up her fingers as she raises it to her chin and starts to play.

All around him, people start to dance. And there's a woman sidling up to Niko, smiling invitingly, her mouth painted bright red. She's standing too close, smiling too wide. There's a flare of heat in Dymitr's chest, harsh and unfamiliar.

Niko's eyes snap to his.

Dymitr doesn't say anything. He just slides his hand into Niko's, nods to the woman—it's not her fault he feels like he might burst into flames, after all—and pulls Niko across the dance floor with a little more force than is necessary.

Niko, for his part, lets himself be pulled, weaving through the crowd of dancers and then tripping up the concrete stairs behind Dymitr. They leave the thump of the music behind. Outside, on the sidewalk, the rusałkas are done with their cigarette, and all the other stragglers have gone inside to listen to the music and let the banshee's song crack them open. Some people like to feel more, like to feel *too much,* but Dymitr doesn't see the appeal. He feels too much already.

He puts a hand on the back of Niko's neck and kisses him hard, tasting beer on his lips and feeling the scratch of day-old facial hair against his chin. Niko's arm wraps around his waist and tugs him closer.

The ache in Dymitr's chest feels distant, now; he's awash in other sensations. His ears are ringing from the loud music; his ears are ringing from the blood thundering through his body. He tastes beer; he tastes Niko's lemon-flavored lip balm. He leans closer, runs his hands over Niko's shoulders, and thinks about what it would be like to peel away each layer of his clothing, one by one.

Niko's teeth graze Dymitr's lower lip, and he makes—a sound, raw and desperate. Niko's hand has come up to Dymitr's chest. Dymitr remembers how Niko's hands look when he transforms, fingernails turning into talons, and a thrill of something that isn't quite fear travels down his spine, his instincts screaming danger and the rest of him calling it nonsense. Niko would never hurt him.

He proved that days ago, in the weapons room with Dymitr's mother.

Dymitr leans closer, and Niko's hand shifts, his thumb, with its sharp strzygoń nail, pressing lightly into the hollow at the base of Dymitr's throat. Niko tries to withdraw it, and Dymitr holds him there with a hand on his wrist.

"I'm not afraid of you, you know," Dymitr says.

"Well, that makes sense, since I find myself incapable of hurting you on purpose," Niko says, in a whisper, right up against Dymitr's mouth. "But I still am what I am. You should remember that before you become . . . attached to me."

"It's far too late for that."

"Is it, now."

Dymitr swallows hard. He nods.

"Is that why you were jealous of that woman?" Niko says, grinning. "The sensation was—quite forceful."

His smile is a half-feral thing. Dymitr likes it.

"Maybe," he says.

"What happened to not being jealous because you're not entitled to me?"

"I'd like to be entitled to you," Dymitr replies. "Is that all right?"

Niko's eyes are bright as lit coals. His fingers brush over the metal now buried in Dymitr's shoulder. Frowning, he follows the smoothness to the center of Dymitr's back, and then down his spine in a slow, curious creep of his fingers. Dymitr shudders, and it's not from the cold, and it's not from the memory of the sword melting into his body again.

"Yeah," Niko says to him. "It is."

A STONE FOR
TWO BIRDS

It's not a long drive to the harbor south of the Loop. They go in Niko's car, where the wind rattles the cloth top, and there's an R.E.M. song—"Drive"—playing over the speakers. The only other car in the parking lot has two teenagers in it, probably about to make out; Niko doesn't linger long enough to find out.

The Razor's sword is in the back seat, wrapped up in cloth. It took some creative magic to smuggle it here on the plane, but Niko's done it before. He's eager to get rid of it. He doesn't like the way he feels in its presence, like his head is stuffed up. It's stifling, somehow.

Niko had to make a plan on the fly, since he never planned to take the sword to begin with—and he doesn't even know why Dymitr told him to. They'll take out the boat that Niko rented from some creature-friendly company—owned by nixies, naturally—and drop the sword in the middle of Lake Michigan. He intended to do it alone, but Dymitr offered to go with him, with a hard look in his eyes that Niko was desperate to understand. So he agreed.

He gets out of the car and reaches into the back seat to pick up the sword. He winces when he touches it, his ears muffled and his head pulsing like a headache without pain. He doesn't bother to lock his door—anyone who wants to break into a cloth-top Jeep just needs a knife and a can-do attitude.

Dymitr is standing at the front of the car, staring at the water. It looks more like an ocean than a lake, here, with the waves rippling in the moonlight, the repetitive sound of them crashing against the rocks. He turns to Niko.

"Can I . . . ?" he asks, and he holds out a hand for the sword.

It means something, Niko thinks, that he doesn't hesitate to hand the weapon over to Dymitr. And he might have, last week. But that was before he saw the lengths to which Dymitr would go to protect Ala, to protect someone who wasn't human.

Dymitr is careful as he unwraps the blade. He closes his hand around the golden handle, and red spills into his palm, red pools in his eyes. Niko steps back, all his instincts screaming at him to transform and attack before he gets attacked himself. But instead of turning away, he forces himself to look. He needs to be honest with himself about what Dymitr is, just as he needs Dymitr to be honest with himself about what Niko is.

"Do you know what will happen to her without it?" Dymitr asks, and it's absurd, to talk to an armed Knight like this.

"I know it'll hurt her, like being separated from your sword hurt you," Niko says. "But beyond that . . . no."

"She'll go mad." Dymitr turns the blade over, studying it. "She'll be haunted by all the creatures she's killed, and then she'll lose her mind."

"Well, I didn't want to be the one who killed your mother, but I'm not going to weep for her."

"I know."

Dymitr sounds strange. Detached. Then he wraps the sword in cloth again, the red receding from his hands, from his eyes. He balances the weapon on his palms, and looks up at Niko, with that same hard expression Niko saw when he insisted on coming along.

"Don't throw it in the water," Dymitr says.

"I'm not going to spare her—"

Dymitr holds up a hand to silence him. "I mean, there's a better use for it."

Niko raises his eyebrows. "And that is . . . ?"

"She'll be able to track it using magic," Dymitr says. "She'll come here, with another Knight, since they almost always travel in pairs. And she'll go wherever the sword is. To a place of your choosing."

Niko catches on, suddenly. "You want me to set a trap."

"Set a trap," Dymitr says. "Use Lidia Kostka as bait so you can save her life. Put her in your debt, so she stops trying to get you killed."

The wind blows the smell of lake water toward them. It shivers through the leaves of nearby trees, and scatters debris across the parking lot. The teenagers in the car at the other end of the lot are leaving now, the bass in their SUV thumping as they pull out onto the street.

Niko stares at Dymitr, who looks steely-eyed and certain. It occurs to him that he's talking not to Dymitr with the soft heart, who wears rumpled shirts and carried Niko's duffel bag through O'Hare Airport because he was tired from the flight . . . but to Dymitr the Knight, who knows his way around a bow and can track any supernatural creature that walks the earth.

"If my trap worked, I would have to kill your mother," Niko says. "Which is the thing you didn't want me to do before."

"I'm aware of that."

"And you're okay with it, suddenly?"

Dymitr looks out at the water again.

"In the weapons room, before you came," he says softly, "she cut into me twelve times. Each time, I begged her for mercy. It only made her cut deeper."

Niko can feel Dymitr's rage, like swallowing a mouthful of high-proof brandy. It burns all the way down, and settles in Niko's stomach like a warm meal.

"I thought I knew what she was. But I didn't." Dymitr swallows hard, his Adam's apple bobbing painfully. "That was my mistake. But I won't make it again."

Niko considers this. Dymitr looks . . . decided. It's the way he looked when he knelt before Baba Jaga and asked her to destroy him. Niko may not know Dymitr that well, but he knows that he's not careless with his words. If he says something has changed . . . it's changed.

As for the idea of using the sword to lure Marzena in, well, it's Niko's preferred strategy. To choose the place where he faces the Knight. To set a trap. To control the surroundings, to watch his quarry's approach. And using Lidia Kostka as bait would certainly solve the problem of her trying to get him killed.

But there's also the small matter of Marzena Myśliwiec being *the Razor*.

"When I fought her before," Niko says slowly, "I barely survived it. I'll be honest—I'm not eager to do it again."

"This time will be different." Dymitr looks him in the eye. "This time, you'll have me."

Niko takes the sword from Dymitr, and sets it down on the hood of the Jeep. He steps in close, grabs Dymitr by the chin, and kisses him hard.

The moon glimmers on the lake. The night is just beginning.

ACKNOWLEDGMENTS

It was such a joy to return to these characters and their world. Thank you to everyone who read and loved (and talked about!) *When Among Crows*. As I've no doubt said before, it takes a village to make a book, and I'd like to thank as many people in mine as I can. So thank you . . .

Lindsey Hall, for saying "Hell yes!" to another Dymitr/ Ala/Niko story and for helping me get it in tip-top shape. Aislyn Fredsall and Hannah Smoot, for the same (and for keeping me on track!). Zan Romanoff, for your thoughtful feedback and our excellent brainstorming sessions.

Joanna Volpe and Jordan Hill, my agent ports in a storm. I'm glad to weather it with you.

At Tor: Rachel Taylor, Eileen Lawrence, Emily Mlynek, Sarah Reidy, Harper Bullard, Stephanie Sirabian, Megan Barnard, Andrew Beasley, Becky Yeager, Yvonne Ye, Rafal Gibek, Dakota Griffin, Steven Bucsok, Michelle Foytek, Alex Cameron, Lizzy Hosty, Erin Robinson, Alexa Best, Will Hinton, Claire Eddy, Christina Mac-Donald, Kyle Avery, Marielle Issa, Lucille Rettino, and Devi Pillai. All of you give these novellas such a wonderful home.

Elishia Merricks and everyone else at Macmillan Audio who worked on the audiobook. Special shout to the voice actors who brought it to life: Helen Laser, James Fouhey, and Tim Campbell.

Katie Klimowicz, Shreya Gupta, Heather Saunders, for making this book so beautiful, inside and out. And of course, Eleonor Piteira, whose amazing art has graced both covers. I'm very lucky.

At New Leaf: Lindsay Howard, Kwali Liggons, Tracy Williams, Keifer Ludwig, Sarah Gerton, Hilary Pecheone, Eileen Lalley, Kim Rogers, Joe Volpe, Donna Yee, Gabby Benjamin, and Katherine Curtis. You all give me such a wonderful home in publishing.

Kristin Dwyer, for your continued enthusiasm and expertise. Molly Mitchell, for the same. Adele Gregory-Yao, for being a little island of order in the chaotic sea of my brain.

Magdalena Chuchro, for being a big help with all things Polish. Courtney Summers, for being such a smart and enthusiastic reader when I needed one. S, Maurene, Sarah, Laurie, Kaitlin, Amy, Kate, Michelle, Kara, Diya, Jen, Morgan, and all the other writers in my life. All the authors who offered *When Among Crows* their blurbs (and all other sources of enthusiasm!). My family, for supporting me.

One of the things this series has done for me is helped me to connect to other people with Polish heritage, whether more distant than mine or far closer. Sometimes this is humbling, as I realize how much I don't know, so a big dziękuje for being patient with my mistakes and for celebrating this wonderful folklore with me.

ABOUT THE AUTHOR

Nelson Fitch

VERONICA ROTH is the #1 *New York Times* bestselling author of the Divergent series (*Divergent, Insurgent, Allegiant,* and *Four: A Divergent Collection*), the Carve the Mark duology (*Carve the Mark, The Fates Divide*), the collection of short fiction *The End and Other Beginnings, Chosen Ones, Arch-Conspirator, When Among Crows,* and many short stories and essays. She lives in Chicago.